FINNY

and the Boy from Horse Mountain

FINNY
and the Boy from Horse Mountain

ANDREA YOUNG

Sky Pony Press
New York

Sky Pony Press books may be purchased in bulk at special discounts for sales promotion, corporate gifts, fund-raising, or educational purposes. Special editions can also be created to specifications. For details, contact the Special Sales Department, Sky Pony Press, 307 West 36th Street, 11th Floor, New York, NY 10018 or info@skyhorsepublishing.com.

Sky Pony® is a registered trademark of Skyhorse Publishing, Inc.®, a Delaware corporation.

Visit our website at www.skyponypress.com.

10 9 8 7 6 5 4 3 2 1

Library of Congress Cataloging-in-Publication Data

Young, Andrea (Andrea Margery), 1963-
Finny and the boy from Horse Mountain / Andrea Young.
    pages cm
 Summary: Fourteen-year-old Finny acquires a horse without her parents knowledge and enlists the help of young Joe, a runaway, to help her train to compete in horse shows, but Joe is kidnapped and it is up to Finny and her horse, Sky, to save him.
  ISBN 978-1-62087-682-4 (hardcover : alk. paper) [1. Horses--Training--Fiction. 2. Runaways--Fiction. 3. Family life--California--Fiction. 4. Kidnapping--Fiction. 5. California--Fiction.] I. Title.
 PZ7.Y8453Fin 2013
 [Fic]--dc23
                    2012050784

Printed in the United States of America

This book is dedicated to the horse world's unsung heroes, the school horse. Without their giant hearts and gentle souls no rider great or small would exist.

Acknowledgments

Special thanks to: My manager and friend, Bonnie Burns, my literary agent, Colleen Mohyde, my editor, Lilly Golden, and to my friends Janice Leonard and Diane Fadok for your support and encouragement Without you ladies my dream never would have come true. Thanks, also, to Lisa Dearing for her stunning photograpic image on the cover. And lastly a giant thank you to my darling student Ivey Burns and her giant Thoroughbred Duke for gracing the cover of my book.

FINNY

and the Boy from Horse Mountain

Chapter One

———

WITH A SOLID BANG THE DOORS SLAMMED shut. The bus rumbled away, leaving Finny in a cloud of gray dust and choking exhaust. She took a long look at the desolate surroundings. Two thoughts crossed her mind: One, no one knew she was here, and two, if her mom found out what she was doing, she was so dead.

Typical for July in California, the temperature was over a hundred and Finny was beginning to sweat. Not just from heat and not just because she had lied to her mom; plain and simple, she was scared. After a deep breath to steady her nerves, Finny started walking.

Crazy Chester was leaning against his rotting wooden porch when Finny came down the dirt drive. His horse, soon to be hers, stood quietly by his side. Finny was afraid of Crazy Chester. All the kids were; his name scared them off, which probably was the point.

Chester handed Finny the lead rope, turning away to hide the tears in his eyes. "He's got the blood of champions running through him, girl, remember that."

Geez, he's old, Finny thought of Chester. She wasn't sure how old. Somewhere near a hundred was her guess, but she wasn't that good at aging old people.

The old man patted the big bay horse's neck. He didn't want to give up his horse, or his home. But like his horse, Chester was thin, malnourished, and neglected. His house, little more than a shack, was falling down. The county intervened, then, finally, his family.

Chester didn't seem crazy to Finny now, and it broke her heart to see him cry. She hadn't thought really old people cried. She thought they had life so figured out that nothing made them sad anymore.

"I promise I'll give him a super good home. I work at Silver Spur Equestrian Center. I know all about horses and how to take care of them."

"That's good, girl. I know you'd treat him right, could tell soon as I saw ya." Finny had told Chester her name was Josephine, or Finny for short, but he continued to call her "girl" anyway.

"His father was blazing fast, girl, blazing fast, unbeatable on the track, set to be the next Seabiscuit, no question about it." Finny watched Chester grow young as he spoke.

"His first race . . . won by three lengths, second race, seven, by the third, people were showin' up just to see him. I had the jockey hold him back, didn't want everyone to know what we had. That's strategy, girl. It's not just fast horses that win races." Crazy Chester tapped his crooked finger to his temple. "You gotta be smart. Sky's father won that race by four lengths, jockey said he wasn't even trying." Chester's young eyes dimmed. "The fifth was the end. I'd like to think it wasn't by a man's hand and it was an act of God, but I'll never know for sure. When a one-in-a-million horse shows up, it gets some people nervous. Throws things out of kilter. Suddenly what was a great horse no longer measures up." Chester gave a small sad shake of his head, his faraway look still deeply vested in the past.

"Bell rang and the gate stuck half open. All thousand pounds of him crashed into it. The horse jammed half through then thrashed and fought to get loose. The jockey jumped clear, but the horse, in a panic, flipped. By the time we got the gate opened and him free, it was too late. His leg was broke." Chester took a deep breath, then a handkerchief from his pocket and dried his eyes. "Saddest day of my life. Doc said there was nothing they could do . . . a part of me died with him that day."

Finny's eyes stung hot trying hard not to cry when Chester looked her way.

"Sorry, girl, got lost in the past. Just wanted to let you know about your horse and where he's from."

"Please tell me everything, if you don't mind." The moment Finny had laid eyes on the horse her heart went out to him. He carried a regalness that defied his pitiful condition.

"Not at all, girl, not at all." Chester cleared his throat and readjusted his thin backside on the porch. "So, that was the end of an era for my wife and me, God rest her. I'd planned after a few years of racing to retire him to stud. He could pass on his lightning speed and we could sit back and collect the stud fees, but of course that never happened. . . . Well, we didn't know it happened. Turned out the little rascal, not even three years old, had jumped the fence into the neighbor's pasture. This neighbor had champion warmblood jumping horses. I'm talking World Cup horses, best money can buy. The next morning the groom found him and walked him over and put him back in our corral. He didn't know my horse wasn't a gelding so he never mentioned it to anyone. But as months passed, my neighbor noticed his most prized horse, his World Cup–winning mare, kept gaining weight. Sick with worry, he had the vet out only to find out she's pregnant." A big crooked smile crossed Chester's face, making Finny smile too.

"So, my neighbor calls me up and, after talking to

the groom, we figured out what happened. I tell you, girl, he was beyond mad. If steam could come outta ears it would've been doing it then. His warmblood that was scheduled to fly to Europe to compete in the Olympic trials had to stay home to have a thoroughbred's baby." Chester slapped his thigh and laughed like it happened yesterday. "I was thrilled to have a part of my great horse alive, but as a thoroughbred-warmblood cross he'd never race, and my neighbor only had purebred warmbloods. He had no use for a cross, but I didn't mind. When Sky was weaned, the groom brought him here and he's been with me ever since."

Finny traced her fingers lightly down the horse's soulful face. Kind, intelligent eyes looked back at her. "I understand why you think he's destined to be a champion."

"It's not just his mom and pop, girl. This horse is all heart, all heart." Chester began to choke up again. Finny tried to steer him back to things positive.

"So, you call him Sky?"

"I named him that 'cause the sky's the limit for this horse. I bet there ain't nothing he can't do."

"Wow, great name. How old is he?"

"Heavens, going on twelve by now I guess."

"Oh, that's not too old. How is he to ride?"

"Don't know, never broke him. By the time he was

old enough, my wife had passed, I'd gotten sick, and next thing I know my kids are making me move into some concentration camp they're passing off as a retirement village." Chester gave a pained chuckle at his statement, not bitter, just resolved.

"Sorry."

"It's okay, girl. I'm glad Sky here has someone now who can get him trained up. He'd never race, but I bet, like his momma, he could jump and if he has half the speed of his papa, well . . . the sky's the limit."

"Thanks, Chester, thanks for letting me have him. I won't let you down."

"I asked at the feed store about you. They told me you'd treat him right and that's what matters to me."

"I will, I promise."

"Okay, girl. Good luck. Sky, prove me right." Chester gave his final pat, then climbed the stairs to his porch and went into his house.

As hard as it was on Chester, Finny wanted to get Sky gone as fast as she could. On the road and around the corner, the horse stopped and looked back. It occurred to Finny that at twelve years old, since he wasn't broke and Chester was elderly, this most likely was the first time he'd ever left the property. Finny stroked Sky's face, then pulled again, urging him to follow. Other than not wanting to go, he wasn't fighting her.

Now out of Chester's sight, Finny gave the horse a more objective once-over. He was very tall, over seventeen hands, dark, dark bay without a white mark on him. He was also painfully thin and had several bald patches across his back and hindquarters, and a huge solid knot for a tail.

Sky, still looking toward his home, nickered softly, breaking Finny's heart. She knew taking him was for the best, but Chester was all he'd known and she was sure Sky loved him.

A few gentle tugs got him moving again. It was getting late. Her original plan had been to ride him home. At a trot or gallop the eleven miles could be made in an hour or so. Finny hadn't known Sky wasn't broke and in such bad shape. At the rate they were moving, it'd be dark before they got back.

It was unlikely her mom would be mad if she were late. Probably wouldn't notice. Finny's twin half sisters, just four, kept her very busy.

Sky tugged at Finny's arm. She found he was like a huge puppy seeing the world for the first time. Sky wasn't afraid of the new things. He stalled at a trash can left by the side of the road for pickup. Finny was certain he'd spook but instead he dragged her to it and dunked his head in. After a laugh and a firm pull she was able to get his head out of the fascinating trash can and get him moving again. She was quickly falling in love.

Now out of the neighborhood, the pair stayed off the road and used the trails through the fields. The roads would have been faster, but introducing the horse to noisy, fast-moving cars would come when Finny knew him better. If he were to spook and bolt, stopping him would be impossible.

Up ahead was a road they'd have to cross, but it was narrow and rarely traveled. Once to it, however, Finny saw a car coming. She moved Sky back and waited for the car to pass.

To her horror, she saw the driver was Elsa, a girl she knew from Silver Spur. Elsa could always find something mean to say under the best of circumstances. With nowhere to hide, Finny braced herself and hoped Elsa would have more interesting things to do than to torment her.

The fancy red convertible, Elsa's sweet-sixteen birthday present, squealed to a stop. Elsa's jaw literally dropped. Her life, Finny realized, must bore her to tears.

Elsa didn't say a word. She just slowly shook her head and motioned to her friends in the car to look. Elsa's passengers, Clara and Shasa, who also rode at Silver

Spur, began to laugh. Then Elsa did, and her laughter continued to grow until she clutched her midsection. Sky decided Elsa's car was so interesting he wouldn't move past it.

"Finny, seriously, that mangy bag of bones is the horse you've been telling everyone about? Your dream horse? God, way to dream big, Finny. It's so pathetic I don't have the heart to insult you."

"You're right, you are totally heartless, Elsa. I couldn't agree more." Finny gave Sky a firm tug and much to her relief he began to follow her across the road and away from the laughter.

"You think you can insult me, trailer trash?" Elsa shouted.

Finny ignored her and kept walking.

"I'm going to tell Jeff right now that if your diseased bag of bones steps on the property, putting my horses at risk, I'm moving them all immediately."

Finny didn't react—she just kept walking, not wanting to let Elsa know she was getting to her. Jeff Hastings, her boss and Elsa's trainer, would never jeopardize his relationship with his high-profile client with four show horses to stand up for a lowly working student.

The little sports car raced off, spitting dust and gravel as it went. Finny knew without a doubt that the gates at Silver Spur would be locked by the time she arrived.

Up ahead on the trail, Finny spotted a small scrub oak that had blown down. She used it to sit and rest, then let some slack out on the lead so Sky could graze. Finny dropped her chin in her hand. She didn't know what to do with a hungry, tired giant of a horse and nowhere to put him. On top of that, it would be getting dark soon.

Calling home wasn't an option—never in a million years. Finny wished she knew why her mom was so against anything horse. Just this morning she had grumbled, "Finny, can't you find something to do that doesn't ruin your clothes and keep you from making friends?"

Frustrated, Finny wiped at the tears dampening her cheeks. She wondered why someone like Elsa, who had everything a teenage girl could want, chose to be so mean.

Trailer trash, Finny thought, I don't even live in a trailer anymore. . . . Finny jumped up and pulled on Sky's lead, urging him to follow her. She had an idea. Changing course, she headed to the end of town, to her old home.

The screaming had started two days after Finny's eighth birthday. She was playing with her new Breyer horse when the fight began. She cantered her plastic horse across the carpet and closed her bedroom door. This was just another fight, or so she thought. Fifteen minutes later the front door slammed and her dad, whom Finny worshiped, walked out of her life.

With a shake of her head Finny forced out old memories and continued to plan. The sun had passed the horizon but left plenty of light. She slowed her pace, wanting it to be dark when she walked Sky into the trailer park. Sky, she noticed, was walking slower and slower, sometimes even staggering. It wasn't hard to burn daylight.

Finny patted Sky's neck and felt the sheen of sweat coating his body. The long walk was taking a toll on him.

It was sufficiently dark when they arrived at the trailer park. Finny heaved a sigh of relief when she found the trailer her mom had been trying to rent, empty. She brought Sky around back, opened a chain link fence made to keep in dogs, and led him through. After a quick inspection of the fence she was confident enough to let Sky off the lead. She hoped the grass in the yard would be enough to keep him busy overnight. Finny found an old trash can, cleaned it, and filled it with water. Sky came over and sniffed the can, then took a long drink. She hated leaving him in a strange place, but she had to get home and he seemed to be content. Finny gave Sky a pat and set off.

* * *

The porch was dark when Finny climbed the stairs and tiptoed into the house. Down the hall she heard the TV. She peeked into the living room and found her mom, Beth, and stepdad, Steven, cuddling on the couch. They were engrossed in a movie with the twins snuggled in between them. They looked good together, like the happy family they were. She thought about her dad. He, too, was remarried with a four-year-old son and two-year-old daughter. His new wife liked the four of them to dress alike. Not identical clothes but in the same colors and styles. It was enough to make them look like they belonged to each other, which they did.

Careful not to disturb anyone, Finny climbed the stairs and went into her bathroom. She flipped on the light and looked in the mirror. Big green eyes on a heart-shaped face framed by amber-colored hair stared back. Finny grabbed a washcloth and scrubbed her face. A moment later she had a dirt-covered washcloth in her hand and a clean shiny face in the mirror. She studied her reflection looking for the pretty her mom said was there. Finny knew she wasn't Elsa-pretty with a perfect nose and bright blue eyes, but not many girls were.

After tossing the washcloth aside, Finny picked up one of her unopened bottles of makeup. She didn't know what to do with it, and didn't really much care, either.

Her mom's repeated pleas ran through her head: "If I bought you makeup would you use it? You've got the high school dance in the fall and all sorts of social events coming up. If you want a boy to ask you to a dance, wash the dirt off and put makeup on."

With a tired sigh, Finny put the bottle down and looked again in the mirror. Never once did Elsa go out without flawless makeup or perfect hair. She wondered if it was normal, at her age, not to care about makeup and dances. Maybe in time, when she had a healthy horse to ride and was happy, then she'd care.

Chapter Two

———

PANIC SHOT ADRENALINE THROUGH JOE'S VEINS, letting him run despite the pain. He needed to get far, fast. With no moon, the night was black, making it near impossible to see but perfect for hiding.

Rain had poured all day and, though it wasn't raining now, Joe was soaking wet. The underbrush and the trees in the forest were dripping, and moving through them was as drenching as rain itself.

Without losing sight of the road, Joe moved as far off the highway as he could. Once certain he was hidden, he slumped to the ground and clutched his throbbing knee and prayed it wasn't broken.

The night wasn't cold, but Joe hugged his jacket closed and said a silent prayer. He wiped his eyes and would have liked to blame his wet face on the rain, but he was scared. He didn't know where he was or what to do next.

Sitting very still, hardly breathing, Joe listened. Nothing but crickets, bullfrogs, and other noises from the night. What he didn't want to hear was the sound of a rough-idling, diesel pickup coming back to find him once it was discovered he was gone.

After a deep breath, Joe pushed himself back to his feet. He had to get farther away. Pain shot through his knee in protest. He rubbed his leg and searched through the dark mass of trees. Bears and wolves hunted at night, and he didn't intend to be an easy target.

The underbrush was thick and full of thorns, making it impossible to navigate. If he were to get anywhere, he would have to take a chance and travel by the road.

Mud and a bad leg made getting back up the slope difficult, but Joe made it and found himself next to a railroad crossing. Behind him, lights were nearing, but it was a semi, not a pickup. A loud bell began to clang. A moment later, crossing lights lit up the night. Joe ducked down in the tall grass and scanned the area. The long wooden rails made to block the tracks began to descend. The semi, with air brakes loudly engaging, slowed and eased to a stop at the barrier. Joe saw it was, of all things, a horse trailer. The biggest, most fancy one he'd ever seen. Painted on the side was a horse jumping through a large silver spur. It was a sign, Joe thought; it had to be. From his hiding place he quickly limped toward the rig. There were multiple storage lockers in the front. If any one of them was open he'd be home free. The ringing stopped; Joe knew the truck would soon move. The first door was locked. He looked over. The gates were lifting. The second door was locked, too. The truck powered up. The third handle moved more than the rest but didn't open. The truck began to roll. Joe grabbed with both hands and yanked. The door flew open and Joe jumped in without a second to spare. He closed the door and found himself in complete darkness, but Joe didn't care. The feeling of the truck moving farther and farther away was all he needed.

Chapter Three

———

LIGHT BLUSHED PINK AND BLUE ACROSS THE sky. Finny was up before the sun. After a quick glass of orange juice and a breakfast bar, she headed off to her new horse. The entire two-mile jog to the trailer was filled with worry. What if he had escaped during the night? Where would he go? Would he know how to get back home? Finny was doing her best to stay positive. Don't be a negative ninny Finny, her dad always said, thinking that was funny.

One mile to go. Finny picked up the pace. She had planned to get there early enough to take him out before the neighbors noticed a horse in a yard meant for a dog.

When she arrived, the gate to the yard was still closed. Thank God, she thought as she opened the latch. She was even more relieved when she saw Sky standing there unharmed. Her happiness immediately morphed into dread when she saw the yard. It was destroyed. The ground was completely dug up. The siding on the trailer had large strips torn away. Apparently, Sky, bored with eating grass, worked on the walls. The small porch roof tipped down at a precarious angle, one corner post having been knocked off. Finny hid her face in her hands. How could she ever explain this? She felt warm air on her fingers. When she peeked through them she found Sky standing in front of her, blowing his warm breath on her hands. That instant he was forgiven.

After a quick look to make sure no one was watching, Finny snapped the lead on his halter and brought Sky out as fast as she could. It was still early and Finny was confident she and Sky hadn't been spotted as they made their way out of the trailer park.

Next door to Silver Spur Equestrian Center was a retirement and rescue home for abused and neglected horses. Finny had never met Vel Moore, the owner, but had heard she was a really nice lady who liked kids and loved horses. Finny was going to take a chance, show up on Vel's doorstep, and beg to work off Sky's board. As pitiful as he looked, Finny figured there was a chance.

The hazy coolness of the morning was disappearing as the temperature rose with the sun. Sky barely moved. Finny figured he must have worn himself out running around all night. She looked at his horribly cracked and neglected hooves and hoped it wouldn't hurt him to walk the two miles to the horse rescue.

Patting the horse's low-slung head, she wondered what was going through his mind. If he knew what was happening, was he happy or sad? She stroked him again and told him she was sure there was a champion amidst all those bones.

As much as she loved to ride, Finny lived to jump. When Chester had said Sky's mother was a World Cup horse, her heart had skipped a beat. She pictured them jumping giant oxers at national competitions, Sky fat and shiny with a jump so powerful it'd be like flying without wings. The mere thought gave her chills. Finny longed to compete in horse shows like the other girls. She longed to accomplish great things with horses. Not just to prove to everyone at Silver Spur she was just as good. She needed to prove it to herself.

The Azure Hills sign—depicting beautiful rolling green hills dotted with shiny horses—was in view. In California the hills were green for only a few weeks in spring. Azure Hills was still beautiful, but its rolling hills were gold.

With a firm shove, Finny opened the gate that hung from the one working hinge. She hadn't considered what to do if the lady said no. *She can't say no*, Finny told herself, tying Sky's lead to the hitching post. She walked to the house and knocked on the door.

"Hello," Vel Moore said, after pushing open her screen door. Finny saw right away Vel wasn't Chester-old. In her forties was her guess, with sun-weathered skin, typical of a lifelong horse-person. Gray in her hair, which wasn't colored because there was feed to buy and stalls to clean, made her look older than she was.

"Yes, um, my name is Finny, and I got a horse and nowhere to keep him. I was sorta wondering if I could work here for his board?"

"Well, this is a first." Vel looked genuinely surprised by the request.

"Sorry to bother you so early."

"No problem, I was up. How old are you?"

"Fourteen, almost fifteen." Vel pondered Finny's request, fingers drumming her hip. "I could use some help, to tell you the truth." Vel, looking over Finny's shoulder, spotted Sky. "Oh my." She came out of her house and down the steps to check out the horse.

"This is Sky. I got him yesterday. . . . They won't let me take him next door like I planned." Vel eyed Sky before turning her attention back to Finny. "This horse is going to need a lot of care, and veterinary attention, and his feet—they're a mess. He's going to take more than work. He's going to take money."

all rescues. I have my two retired horses and an old pony that's blind in the pasture next to them. The pony was a rescue, too."

"Poor pony. He's okay with other horses?"

"He sure is. He's the boss out there. I'll show you what I mean." Vel took a carrot from her pocket and led Finny out of the barn toward the back of the property. Finny could see Azure Hills ended at the base of the mountain just like Silver Spur.

Vel's pastures were laid out in a U shape. Two small pastures bordered the north and south sides of the property. The biggest pasture was the entire back five acres. Vel let out a loud cluck. The pony instantly lifted his head from the grass and made his way toward the noise. The two horses with him followed.

"See how the horses stay back."

"Wow, he's half their size. What's his name?" Finny reached over the fence, talking to the mostly white little Appaloosa pony. She saw his eyes were cloudy and didn't want to scare him.

"His name is Buster. He was a Silver Spur school pony for close to twenty years until he went blind. This pony has safely taught hundreds of kids to ride. He's given so much joy over the years, I think he deserves a nice retirement." Vel lovingly stroked the pony's spotted neck.

"How did you get him?" Finny was surprised Vel had one of Jeff's ponies.

"I got a frantic call from one of Silver Spur's old students. She heard Buster left on a trailer to go to the slaughter yard. She begged me to help, and, well, here he is."

"Oh," was all Finny could think to say. She couldn't believe Jeff Hastings, who she so respected, could do such a thing, especially to a pony that had served him so well for so many years.

"The other two are Max and Stella. They're my horses. They're both well into their twenties now." Vel had a big smile on her face when she handed them both carrots. The horses gently took them from Vel's hands and nosily ate them.

"They're beautiful, Vel." As elderly as they were, Finny could see from their conformation the two warmbloods, both gray, must have been lovely in their prime.

Finny was introduced to the remaining herd. Vel described the care each horse needed and then Finny followed her back to the barn, where they sat down to write up a list of daily chores. Finny was relieved that the list looked easy to accomplish. She'd help with the stall cleaning, grooming, and medicating the horses that needed it in the evening. It'd be a breeze.

Finny gave Sky, who was picking at his hay, a pat

good-bye before she had to go to Silver Spur to work. She washed her hands, about scrubbing her skin off, then slid through the fence and went next door.

It was like stepping into a different world. Silver Spur had twenty-five green, beautifully irrigated acres peppered with giant oak trees. The fences surrounding the property and dividing all the pastures were gleaming white. The two large pastures at the front of the property were bisected by a long cobblestone-edged driveway lined with maple trees that led to the main barn. No expense had been spared when the grand brick fifty-stall barn was built, designed to look like a country estate, complete with manicured courtyard. People new to the farm were often surprised to walk through large ornate doors only to find horse stalls instead of bedrooms.

Finny hurried through the front pasture to the driveway. She still got a thrill every time she walked up to the beautiful barn. Centered in front of the barn was the main outdoor jumping arena. This was Jeff's private arena and he only let his top riders use it. As a working student, paying for lessons only with her labor, that ring had been off limits. But, last year Jeff had told Finny she was riding so well that she should join the advanced lessons. That had been a turning point for Finny. For the most part, she had been ignored by the other girls, who paid large lesson fees to Jeff and big bucks to board their horses at Silver Spur. After her first lesson with them, several became openly hostile. They didn't want a lowly working student riding with them on their level. Her participation in those lessons didn't last long.

Finny jogged up the aisle that divided the main barn from the large indoor ring. She could feel the give of the rubber non-slip floors that were specially designed to look like bricks. All the ornate brass stall nameplates and halter holders in the barn sparkled in the sunlight that streamed in through the large skylights.

Once through the barn and out the other side, the structures were more simple. Made for usefulness, not for show. Finny went to the barn manager's office. Ray wasn't there, nor was the head groom, Carl, Ray's brother.

Finny saw the clipboard with her duties for the day. She gasped at the amount of work she was assigned. She took a deep breath, then the paper from the clipboard. Carl had been giving her more and more to do, giving her some of his own duties for that matter. Finny wasn't afraid of hard work. The problem was that she was only human. Once, after a particularly grueling day, she got up the courage to say something to Ray about her workload. He just shook his head with disappointment and told Finny she must not realize what a privilege it was to ride and work at Silver Spur and he was sure he'd find plenty of other people who would happily take her place.

Today, Finny hustled to the tack room. The advanced girls were scheduled to take their lesson at noon. Number one on her list of thirty: All their tack needed cleaning before they arrived.

Finny lined up the four saddles so she could work efficiently. After soaping and polishing the leather she buffed the nameplates. Elsa, Sasha, Olivia, Clara. Jeff's elite riders. "The girls who keep me famous," he called them.

Finny went to work next on Elsa's bridles. She didn't know which of Elsa's four horses she would be riding, so Finny cleaned them all. It had been Elsa, Jeff had told her, who had put an end to Finny's lessons with the elite. Elsa had thrown a fit and Jeff admitted that keeping Elsa happy was a priority since her father bankrolled the whole place.

When the bridles were spotless, Finny jogged to get to item two on her list: Washing the training pads and polo wraps. Next to the feed storage was the laundry room with two industrial-size washing machines and dryers as well as a utility sink and storage cabinet. Finny took the sack leaning up against the machine with all the pads and shoved them into the washer. Shouting outside caught her attention. She quickly shut the washing machine and peered out the door to see what was going on.

Ray was cursing up a storm from inside Silver Spur's horse trailer. He came out of the storage room dragging a man out behind him.

"Carl, check the trailer, make sure nothing's missing. I just caught us a thief." Carl, who also helped with the cross-country drives, ran into the rig and checked all the equipment.

Finny looked around to see if anyone else was there to witness the scene happening behind the barn. She didn't see Jeff anywhere, or anyone else, for that matter.

"Everything's there. Just found this." Carl held up a backpack. The man, who was no match for Ray's six-foot-two, broad-as-a-barn frame, struggled to get out of his grip. Finny saw then that it wasn't a man. It was a teenage boy.

"Check the bag." Ray growled to his brother without loosening his hold on the teenager.

"Why were you in our truck?" Ray asked the boy with a hard shake.

"I saw you were a horse ranch. I . . . need a job."

"I think I did find something that was stolen." Carl said. He pulled out a handful of money from the backpack.

"Hey, that's mine!"

"Good thing I found him, Carl. We don't need no thief here." Ray wore a telling smile.

"Where did you get on, kid?"

"Give me my money." The boy grabbed for his backpack. Carl easily kept it from his reach.

"Had to be Phoenix, that was the last time we stopped for gas."

"You're in California, boy. What do you expect us to do with you now?"

"Let me go." Realizing it was useless, the boy stopped fighting the big man. He looked up and locked eyes with Finny for a brief moment. Carl gave the boy his backpack minus the money.

"Get him off the property, Carl. Kid, if I see you again, I ain't gonna be so nice."

From behind the barn door, Finny watched the boy being driven away. She contemplated telling Jeff that Ray and Carl had stolen a kid's money, but would he care about some stowaway? Carl and Ray were Jeff's trusted go-to guys. They'd deny it and Finny knew she'd probably end up being kicked out. With a heavy heart, she went back to work.

Finny was feeling sore and very tired by the time she slid through the fence into Azure Hills.

Vel was nailing up a new board on a stall to replace one a horse had broken. She worked to hold it straight and drive the nail home but was having trouble getting the board and nail to cooperate. Finny grabbed the board and steadied it.

"Thanks," Vel said. She looked even more tired and disheveled than Finny.

"No problem." Three hammer hits later the board was secured.

"Finny, I was thinking . . . With your help, I could take on some boarding horses and maybe generate some income. Do you think you can stay on during the school year?"

"I can. Tell me what you need and I'm there."

"Will you have enough time?"

"Yes, I totally will." As tired as she was, Finny meant every word.

"Wonderful, it would help so much. I've been fighting to keep this place open. Donations are down thanks to the bad economy, and my paycheck only goes so far."

"Oh no, this place can't close. What would happen to the horses?"

"I don't know. That's why I'm trying so hard."

"I'll get to work right now. What do you need?"

Vel gave a laugh. "I just finished. I had today off so I

put my time to good use. I called the vet for you. He'll be here tomorrow morning."

"Thank you so much. I'll be here first thing tomorrow morning. I'll feed the horses and clean all the stalls before I go next door. I really appreciate you letting Sky stay here."

"It's my pleasure, and a day off from barn chores sounds like heaven."

"Oh, could I use your phone? My mom's picking me up and I want to tell her I'm here and not at Silver Spur."

"Sure, honey, it's in the kitchen."

After five rings Finny's mom picked up the phone with a rushed hello.

"Hey mom, just wanted to tell you I'm at Azure Hills, not Silver Spur. What time are you coming?"

"Your dad's picking you up today."

"No, they went out of town, remember?"

"What? He didn't tell me that."

"I did a week ago."

"Your father needs to communicate with me directly. Please remind him of that."

"Okay, so are you coming?"

"I just put the girls in the tub. You'll have to wait until they're done."

"Mom, that'd be forever. Can't Steven come get me or something?"

"He's busy in the den with a project from work. Could you walk, sweetheart? It'd help me out so much."

"But it's almost dark."

"Then stay on the trails and off the roads. It's not that far. Come on, Finny, you've walked it a million times."

"Fine, I'll walk."

"Thanks, baby. See you soon."

By the time Finny was saying good-bye the dial tone was humming in her ear.

Four miles by road, five or so by trail. Finny stayed on the road to get home faster. She could have jogged but it was still hot and she was already exhausted from working all day. Being forgotten yet again didn't help anything either.

At the highway, Finny checked both directions before running across. Once on the other side, a semi truck whizzed by, giving Finny a slight shove with a warm blast of air as it covered her in a cloud of dust. Being a little too close for comfort, Finny moved farther off the road and walked along the typically bone-dry concrete California flood control channel. After about a mile, she spotted the bus stop shelter. The shelter didn't catch her eye, but the person sitting behind it did. It was the boy she had seen earlier getting kicked out of Silver Spur.

The bus would go right by; the driver would never see him back there. When she got closer Finny saw he was asleep.

"Hey, wake up." Her words had no effect. Finny noticed his eye and cheek were purple and his lip was split. She gently shook his shoulder. The boy jerked awake. After a moment of disorientation, Joe remembered where he was and gazed up at Finny.

"You're going to miss your bus back here."

Joe looked for his backpack, found he'd been lying on it, and picked it up.

"Did Carl do that to you?" Finny motioned to his face and saw that besides having a black eye and split lip he was sweating profusely. She didn't know what to think when he closed his eyes without answering. Finny looked up and down the road then back to the teenager. She shook him awake again. He was hot to the touch.

"I think you need a doctor."

Joe shook his head.

The sun had set, dropping the temperature to a reasonable eighty-five. Finny rubbed her forehead.

"What's your name?"

"Joe," he said, then closed his eyes again.

"I think I better call an ambulance."

"No, I'm okay." Joe struggled to rouse himself as if to prove it.

"It's almost seven. I don't think the next bus comes until tomorrow morning."

"I'm not waiting for the bus. I just need to rest a little." Joe touched his split lip. Speaking had made it bleed again.

"What happened? I saw you drive away with Carl."

"I tried to get my money back." Using his T-shirt Joe blotted the blood from his lip.

"You should call the police."

"No," Joe shook his head. "I just got to somehow get it back."

"How much did you have?"

"Little over three hundred."

"Carl's a real jerk."

Joe hugged his backpack and slumped back against the wall.

"Is there anyone you can call for help?"

Joe looked at Finny for a moment before giving an almost indiscernible shake of his head.

For the third time Finny glanced up and down the road, as if that action would lead to an answer. The boy seemed as pitiful as Sky. Finny wanted to help him now, since she hadn't been able to help him earlier.

"Do you think you can walk a little over a mile?"

Joe looked confused at the question.

"If you can, I have a place for you to stay. It's where I used to live. There's a bed and everything. No food but I could bring some." Joe quietly studied Finny for a moment.

"Why would you help me?"

The question caught Finny by surprise.

"Why wouldn't I help you?"

Joe ran his hand through his thick dark hair. He had no answer.

"It's a mobile home. Me and my mom used to live there. Electricity and water are still on and everything." Finny watched what must have been the wheels spinning in his head.

"Come on, twenty-minute walk tops. You can sleep there tonight, then deal with getting your money back tomorrow." Finny felt a kinship for the boy, although if pressed wouldn't have been able to come up with why. She offered a hand to help him up. After a pause Joe took it and then stood. Once on his feet, he dug through his backpack and pulled out a hat, shook it, and did his best to get the old worn felt cowboy hat back in a reasonable shape before snugging it down on his head.

"It's this way." Finny motioned down the road. Joe nodded and followed.

Finny watched him out of the corner of her eye. He

was taller than her five-eight and on the thin side. His T-shirt and jeans were old and stained. The backpack he carried was dark green and had an Army insignia on it. Finny couldn't help but notice underneath the dirt and sweat he had soft brown eyes and a pleasantly handsome face . . . along with a pretty decent limp.

"Thank you," Joe said after a few minutes of walking in silence.

"No problem." Finny gave him a smile. Between how sick he looked and his limp, she hoped he'd make it.

"Do you know anyone hirin' around here? I'm good with horses." He spoke with a subtle accent, a soft twang.

"You don't want to go back to Phoenix?"

"I'm not from Phoenix. I need a job anywhere."

"Are you eighteen?"

Joe shook his head.

"Sixteen?"

Joe shook his head again.

"You're fifteen?" Finny asked with surprise.

"Yeah, wish I looked older. Be easier gettin' a job."

"Did you run away from home?"

After a slight pause Joe shook his head no. Finny didn't push. They were almost to the trailer.

"I'll ask at the feed store. They might know who's hiring," Finny told him, but with his limp, he moved pretty slow. She wondered if anyone would hire him in that condition. At the rate they were going it would again be long past dark before she got home.

At the trailer park, the streets were quiet. With mostly older residents, that was typical. Finny unlocked the door and quickly got Joe inside. The trailer was oven hot and stuffy, so she dashed around and opened windows and then turned on a fan. The trailer was still furnished and had most everything a person needed. Finny's mom had wanted a new start with her new husband and left most of the possessions from her first marriage behind. Joe looked around, unsure of what to do. Finny worried about how pale he was.

"Joe, why don't you go sit on the couch. I'll get you some water."

Joe nodded and sank into the soft cushions, then took off his hat and lay it on the coffee table. By the time she was back with his water, Finny thought he had fallen asleep, but his eyes opened when she came into the room. He downed the water immediately after she handed it to him.

"I got to get home. The shower works and we have a washer and dryer. Try not to make it obvious someone's here. I don't think the neighbors would call my mom, but you never know."

Joe nodded.

"There isn't any food, but I'll bring some tomorrow if you want."

"It's really nice of you to help me."

"No problem. I better get going. I'll be here early. I hope you feel better." Finny gave a quick wave, then closed the door behind her.

Joe glanced around the room. With the windows opened and the fan on it was cooling down. He felt his swollen eye and split lip and wished he had some ice. He was dead tired and his knee was killing him. Joe pulled his pant leg up and looked; it was purplish yellow, swollen, and ugly.

The refrigerator was in plain view from where he sat. He'd take a chance and look in the freezer. Pain shot through his leg when he stood, making his head swim. After a moment Joe limped over to the kitchen. He opened the freezer and found a lone bag of peas. It was like a gift from the heavens. He pressed the cold bag to his swollen face. He knew it had been dumb to try to fight Carl. He was no match. It was panic over losing his money that caused him to lose his head. *For all the good it did*, Joe thought miserably.

The cold air from the freezer made him shiver. He could feel heat emanating from his skin. He couldn't believe that on top of everything else, he was sick. Joe limped back to the couch. California . . . unbelievable. It was a lot farther than he thought and that was fine with him. Ray and Carl had been wrong. Joe had been in the truck for almost three days, not less than one.

After balancing the bag of peas on his swollen knee, Joe lay back. Once they thawed, he planned to eat them. He couldn't remember the last time he'd had a solid meal. It'd been two days without any food at all. Joe's eyes grew heavy as he looked around the modest trailer. To him, it looked like paradise.

The porch light burned bright but the rest of the house sat dark. Finny used her key and went inside. After fumbling around she found the light switch. Her stomach got tight when her mom wasn't there waiting for her. Finny reasoned that she was almost fifteen, and her mom must expect her to take care of herself by now.

She opened the fridge and found it jam-packed with food. After shutting the door she ran up the stairs and knocked gently on her mom and Steven's door. Beth stepped out into the hall. "I'm glad to see you're finally home."

"Came as fast as I could. . . . Hey Mom, if you're really sick with a fever, what should you do?"

"Are you sick?" Beth touched the back of her hand to Finny's forehead.

"No, I was just wondering."

"Well, you'd take Tylenol to lower the fever, drink lots of fluids, and rest. That's about all you can do if it's the flu."

"Thanks, Mom."

"Sure, sweetheart." Beth kissed Finny on the forehead, then heard one of the twins holler. She rolled her eyes and took off in that direction.

Back in the kitchen, Finny looked at the leftovers from dinner: pasta with vegetables. She chewed her lower lip and glanced at her watch. Thirty minutes round trip is all it would take by bike. She dashed up to her room and grabbed her backpack. A bottle of Tylenol was in the bathroom; she tossed it in the pack, then grabbed some towels and washcloths before heading back down to the kitchen, where she loaded as much food as she thought she could get away with taking. Finny stepped back and looked. The fridge still looked packed. Finny put the backpack on the porch, then stood in the kitchen and listened for sounds of her mother. She had never snuck out at night before and seriously doubted her mom would notice if she were to leave now. Finny crept out, closed the door quietly, and jumped on her bike.

* * *

Fifteen minutes later she was at the door of the mobile home. When she got no response to her gentle knock, she opened the door. Joe was asleep on the living room couch, a warm bag of peas on his knee. Finny took the bag and put it back in the freezer so he could use it again. As quietly as she could she placed the food in the refrigerator, then contemplated waking Joe so he could take the pills but decided to let him sleep. Finny lightly touched his forehead. He was burning hot. She went back to the kitchen and soaked a washcloth in cool water, then folded it in thirds and placed it on his forehead. Unsure, she watched him for a while. What if he had something worse than the flu? Finny was tempted to call her mom and confess everything. Her sense that Joe wouldn't want that prevented her. She'd give it one more day. If he wasn't better, she'd tell her mom. Finny wrote a quick note to Joe about the food and medicine, then jumped on her bike and took off for home.

Joe woke with a panicked start. He blinked several times and rubbed his eyes. After a moment of bewilderment he remembered where he was. Joe found a washcloth on his forehead. He pulled it off and sat up, scanning the room.

"Hello?" No one answered. Joe saw next to his hat on the coffee table was a bottle of Tylenol and a glass of water with two pills lying next to it. He took the pills and finished off the water.

The full night's sleep had done him good. Joe knew he had a fever and was starving, but he no longer felt exhausted on top of that. He spotted Finny's note telling him she'd brought food. Joe shot off the couch. His knee screamed in protest, stopping him instantly. He waited until the pain eased and the dizziness passed before carefully making his way to the kitchen. With trembling hands he took the food containers out of the fridge and put them on the table. Not bothering with a fork or a spoon, he began to eat with his hands. There was a lot of food. Joe wasn't used to dealing with other kids his age. He was amazed by what a kind girl Finny was.

Twenty minutes later, Joe sat back. His stomach felt like it would burst. He wished he could keep eating. He couldn't remember the last time he'd felt this full, or if he'd ever felt this full. Tired again, Joe limped back to the couch and was out before his eyes closed.

The clock refused to move no matter how many times Finny checked it. She jigged her leg with impatience.

Her mom had surprised the family with pancakes for breakfast. All five of them were having a meal together for the first time in a long time. Her sisters were being adorable, her mom and Steven were happy, and the food was great, but Finny was going nuts. She had a hidden boy and a secret horse to get to.

Finny held out as long as she could before asking to be excused. Her mom, happy with the breakfast, said yes and Finny was out the door again with a backpack full of food and supplies.

Fifteen minutes later she was knocking on the door of the trailer. When she got no response, she opened the door and peered in. Joe was still asleep on the couch. She was relieved to see the half-empty food containers on the table. This meant he hadn't died of some mysterious disease during the night.

Finny lightly touched Joe's forehead. He was definitely cooler. She unloaded more food into the refrigerator from her backpack, then went back to the living room. She didn't want to leave Joe, but she had promised Vel she would clean the stalls and give the medications today. Not to mention the vet was coming for Sky and she had her lesson at Silver Spur. Figuring Joe had a few days of rest ahead of him, she left him with a note explaining where she was and when she'd be back. Finny hopped on her bike and headed for her horse.

* * *

All the horses were fed and eight of the eleven stalls were clean when the vet rolled up. Finny prayed the two hundred dollars of babysitting money she had in her pocket would be enough.

Dr. Scott Monie stepped out of his truck. Finny knew Dr. Monie from her work at Silver Spur and liked him very much. He was in his forties, handsome, with a thick mop of curly dark hair lightly sprinkled with gray. His best feature, though, was a quick-witted sense of humor that kept everyone laughing.

"How you doing there, Finny?"

"Good, Dr. Monie, and you?"

"Right as rain, darling. So what's this I hear? You have a horse?"

"I sure do. He's right this way. He's not in the best shape."

"Well, we'll fix that."

Finny grabbed her lead and halter and went to Sky. Sky stood with his head down in a pile of fresh hay that he wasn't eating. Finny haltered him and led him out of his corral.

"Well, lookie here." Dr. Monie ran a hand down Sky's neck before stepping back and taking in the whole picture.

"You got yourself a project, I'm afraid." Dr. Monie

took his stethoscope from his neck and listened to Sky's heart and lungs. "So far so good. Lungs are clear and no heart murmur."

Finny was overjoyed. The doctor continued the practical exam. "Eyes are good, clear."

He picked up Sky's feet, one at a time, and applied the rounded clamps of the hoof tester on several spots on each hoof. Sky jerked his front hooves away from the tester when Dr. Monie pressed them on the toe area. He didn't mind the pressure on his back hooves at all.

"His front hooves are beginning to abscess," Dr. Monie said, after putting the tester away.

"I had to walk him a really long way. I know he wasn't used to it. Did I hurt him bad?" Finny's heart sank; she hadn't meant to hurt her horse.

"No, sweetheart, he'll be fine. His front hooves are pretty soft but we can fix that."

Next, Dr. Monie moved to Sky's mouth and examined his teeth and gums. "Here's the biggest problem. It doesn't look like his teeth have ever had care. He still has his wolf teeth and he has pockets of infection on his gums. The sharp points on his teeth have cut the inside of his mouth. That's why he's not eating—it hurts too much."

"Can you help him?"

"You bet. Hang on, I'll get my tools."

"Sky, you're going to feel better real soon!" Finny patted Sky's sorrowful face. Dr. Monie came back and got to work. First he sedated Sky, and then with his electric floater he filed away at the big horse's teeth. Fifteen minutes later Sky's teeth were smooth and correct. Next, using a simple pair of surgical pliers, Dr. Monie popped Sky's wolf teeth out and handed them to Finny.

"I can't believe how easily they came out." Finny rolled the funny-looking teeth around in her hand.

"They typically do, but his were infected so that helped."

Dr. Monie sat on the bumper of his truck and went over the list of things Finny needed to do.

"Okay, first of all, he has to be on antibiotics twice a day for ten days, for the infection in his mouth." The doctor handed Finny two large bottles. "Next, he needs to be treated for intestinal parasites every day for five days with these." He handed her five large tubes of dewormer. "Then he should go on a daily wormer with his supplements. This medication here is topical for the ringworm and this drawing salve is for his feet; it will help pull out the abscesses." Dr. Monie handed Finny more bottles and containers than she could hold. She went white just looking at all the medicine, which alone must cost more than two hundred dollars. Dr. Monie noticed her reaction.

"Finny, how much money do you have for the visit?"

"Two hundred."

"Well, that's lucky, 'cause that's exactly what all this comes out to today."

"Are you sure?" she asked, knowing it couldn't be true.

"Yes, I'm sure." He gave Finny a smile when she handed him the money.

"Thanks, Dr. Monie. Thanks for everything."

"Good luck. Call me if you need anything." With that, the doctor got in his truck and headed to his next appointment. Finny was certain he was the nicest man she'd ever met.

Head down and pathetic-looking, Sky was led back to his corral. Finny got his medicine ready, but Sky had no interest in eating anything, much less bitter-tasting medicine. Finny went to the supply cabinet, got a large syringe, and dropped the pills inside. She added water to let the pills dissolve and then put some molasses in to make it sweet. It was a strain to hold his giant head up as she squirted the mixture in his mouth. Luckily, Sky liked the taste and didn't fight her. Finny let his head drop. It went back to almost touching the ground and now he was drooling, too.

Finny stepped back and let out a sigh at his state. She had no regrets but was feeling a bit overwhelmed with all her new responsibilities.

Finny looked for anything she could do for Sky in the few minutes she had left. She fetched the bottle of conditioner she'd brought from home and drenched his tail in it. After a few minutes of massage she could pull some strands free. Happy with her progress, she let Sky's tail soak while she went next door for her lesson.

Elsa was in the ring on one of her zillion-dollar mounts. Jeff was training her. Finny saw Sasha, Clara, and Audrey riding in the field, lessoning with Barbara. Even though those girls were Elsa's friends, she must have wanted Jeff and the main arena to herself today. Finny gave the arena a wide berth so Elsa wouldn't have the chance to taunt her as she walked to the stable.

Tank was the horse written next to Finny's name on the lesson board. She noticed she got the most difficult horse to ride when Elsa was around, and she was pretty sure it was Elsa's handwriting on the board. Finny went into the tack room and grabbed a halter. Tank was a handful on a good day, but, unbeknownst to Elsa, Finny didn't mind. She loved the challenge and felt the tougher the horse was, the better the rider it made.

She grabbed Tank from a back pasture and led him back to the barn to tack up. Finny wondered about Joe and hoped he was okay.

Jeff was scheduled to teach her group today. When Finny found out, her nerves went on overdrive. She loved her lessons with Barbara, because she kept them fun and challenging, but it was thrilling when Jeff taught. He was demanding, tough, and unforgiving, but also the top trainer in the state and riding with him was a rare privilege.

From the moment Finny mounted Tank she could feel tension pulsing through him. He felt like a rodeo bronc ready for the gate to swing open and the fun to begin. Finny headed to the cross-country field where Katie, Kayla, and Ivey were warming up. The three girls were two years younger and not up on barn politics. They were sweet, and Finny knew they looked up to her as a rider so she always tried to do her best and help them when she could.

The only way to the field was to go right by the main ring. Tank jigged under her, tense and wanting to buck. Which he did, right before bolting across the field. Finny managed to get him under control by jerking the rein hard and turning him in a circle, but it was too late. Tank's antics spooked the horse Elsa was on, causing it to spin and dump her hard in the dirt. The next instant a blood-curdling scream cut the air. Jeff and Barbara ran to Elsa, who caterwauled like she was dying. Sasha, Clara, and Audrey trotted their horses over to the rail to see if Elsa was all right. Finny saw Elsa point to her, then gesture wildly. She knew her goose was cooked. She'd be kicked out of the lesson because she couldn't control her horse. Finny saw Barbara look her way and shake her head. Finny nodded and turned Tank back toward the barn. She wanted to cry, but didn't—what was the point?

Back at the crossties, Finny's ears were still ringing. She was sorry Elsa had been thrown, but although she had played a part in it, Finny didn't feel one hundred percent responsible. She also knew Elsa was okay. People who are really hurt don't have the strength to carry on and holler like Elsa was doing.

Because Tank was done for the day and no one else would ride him, Finny gave him an extra long curry and brushing after she untacked him. Audrey and Clara had horses in the next crossties. They chatted amicably to each other while they cared for their horses but ignored Finny as usual. Sasha had her groom taking care of her horse so she sat on the bench watching the other girls work.

Sasha began talking about the upcoming horse show, what classes she was going to compete in, what medals she was going to try to qualify for. The other girls chimed in.

Sasha knew Finny never got to show and how badly she wanted to, so she brought it up every chance she got.

Finny had heard enough, so she led a nicely groomed Tank around the back of the barn. She was undoing Tank's halter to turn him out when she saw someone climbing through the window of the house where Ray and Carl lived. She gasped when she realized it was Joe. She spun around and looked for Ray's truck, grateful it was gone. Finny quickly shut the pasture gate and ran to the open window Joe had just slipped through.

"Joe," she hissed, "Joe!" From the hall, Joe came back into the room. "Have you lost your mind? Get out of there!" Finny looked back over her shoulder, positive Ray and Carl would be back any minute.

"I gotta get my money back. It's all I have."

"Joe, if they come back, you're dead."

"Can you watch for them? Yell if they come." Joe disappeared down the hall.

"Come on, get out of there!"

He didn't answer; Finny heard banging around in the other room. She looked again, scanning the yard for any sign of Carl or Ray. Their house was well hidden by trees and far from the barn, but that didn't ease Finny's fears.

"Joe!" Finny was beginning to panic.

He came back into the room. "I can't find it! What am I gonna do?"

"Carl probably has it on him if he hasn't spent it

already. Please get out of the house." Much to her relief he came to the window and crawled out.

"Geez, I'm gonna sound just like my mother, but what were you thinking?"

"I was thinkin' I'm screwed without my money."

"I'm so sorry." Finny said as she led him away from the house. "We better get out of here. I need to get my stuff, and then we can go next door. Did you walk all the way here?"

"Yeah."

"Your limp looks worse." She also noticed he'd showered and his worn clothes were now clean. "Did you hurt your knee falling from a horse?"

Joe nodded.

"I can ask Vel from next door to give us a ride back to the trailer. She's really sweet. Wait here just a second," Finny told him as they entered the barn. "My stuff's in the tack room."

Finny was glad she didn't have to work on her lesson days. She ran into the tack room and grabbed her bag with her spurs, chaps, and helmet. When she came back outside her whole body went tight. Elsa was standing in front of Joe, talking to him.

"So are you looking for a place to ride?" Elsa asked.

Finny noted the tone of her voice and how she was standing and looking at Joe. She was flirting.

Joe got up from the couch and went for what was left of the food. Finny, not hungry herself, sat with him while he ate. "So about your knee, there's this free clinic in town that can look at it."

"You mean like a free doctor? I didn't know there was such a thing."

"My mom and I used them after she got divorced from my dad. But we'd have to be there early and it'd most likely take all day."

"We? You mean you'd go with me?"

"Well, yeah, if you want."

"Do you think they'd treat me without a parent or ID?"

"At the clinic, they don't ask for ID or anything. It won't be a problem. If they ask how old you are just say eighteen."

"Okay, thanks. And I'll help you more with your horse than just his tail. I'll help you break and train him. If you want my help, I mean."

"Are you kidding? I've broke exactly zero. I would love your help! You're a *Godsend*!" Finny said, quoting Vel. She could see she'd made Joe happy, and that made her happy too.

Chapter Four

———

THE BUS PULLED INTO TOWN AT 8 AM, RIGHT on time. Finny and Joe sat near the back.

"So, how did you really hurt your knee?"

"On a horse."

"From a fall or a kick?"

"Fall."

"You told Vel you were kicked."

"I . . . was. I fell then got kicked."

Finny glanced at Joe. He was staring at the floor. She knew he wasn't telling the truth.

"I think we're almost there."

"Thanks for coming. I've never been on a bus. I would've got lost."

"Sure, no problem." Finny looked away. She thought Joe had wanted her company, not a guide. She took a deep breath and stared out the window. Why did that bother her? She didn't want to be like her mother or most of the girls she knew in school who lived only for boys. Or, in her mom's case, men. After the divorce, it was a struggle even to get her mother out of bed.

She looked at Joe, confused by her feelings, which tumbled around so much when it came to him. She barely knew him. He was a nice guy, a new friend, but that was it. And that was fine with her, she told herself. Besides, she didn't want a boyfriend, and if all he wanted was a bus guide, so be it. The bus rolled to their stop.

"This is it. We're here." Finny got up and went to the door. She waited for Joe, annoyed now by how slow he was. Once on the sidewalk Finny headed off in the direction of the clinic.

"This way," she said. She stood by the clinic door with her arms crossed and her foot tapping.

"Finny, did I do something to make you mad?" Joe said once he'd caught up to her.

"No, you didn't," Finny said with a sigh, feeling stupid.

"I'm sorry you had to come. I didn't know it'd be such a hassle."

"I wanted to come." Finny opened the door and the two walked in to chaos. The waiting room was packed, not a seat available, leaving several people camped out on the floor. The place reeked of urine and the sound of babies crying was deafening.

"Oh, lordy," muttered Joe.

They made their way through the mass of bodies. Once they were at the counter, the obviously harried nurse barked out, "Name!"

"Uh, Joe."

"Last name?"

Joe looked at the nurse, then at Finny.

"Tell her your last name, Joe." Finny put her hands on her hips thinking he'd lie again.

"McCoy . . . Joe McCoy." Finny let her arms drop. That sounded real. After he explained why he was there the nurse gave him a number, then told them they were looking at a four- to five-hour wait.

"Let's go sit outside so we can breathe," Finny whispered.

Joe followed her out. On the lawn more people were camped out. A speaker sitting in a window called out numbers.

"There's a spot under a tree in the shade."

"Race you to it," Joe said, making Finny laugh. They made their way and got comfortable.

"So, is McCoy your real last name?"

"Think I'm lying?"

Finny said nothing.

Joe settled back against the tree. "It's really my name."

"Joseph McCoy. That's a nice name."

"Joseph McCoy. That's my dad's name. Well, *was* my dad's name. I'm just Joe."

"Was . . . did your dad die?"

Joe picked up a small pebble and tossed it. "Yeah, he and my mom, when I was eleven."

"That's awful. I'm so sorry."

Joe continued to toss whatever small pebbles he could find as far as he could.

"What happened?"

"They were driving home and hit black ice. Truck flipped."

"Sorry . . . I wish I knew what to say."

"Nothin' to say." Frustrated when he ran out of rocks, Joe moved to any debris he could find to toss. Finny sat cross-legged next to him and watched him throw stuff. She stayed quiet, leaving Joe with his thoughts. Her mind was wandering when he asked, "What about your parents?"

"My parents . . . well, they're divorced and hate each other." Finny let out a small laugh. "I was eight when they separated. Eleven when my mom married Steven. My dad got remarried too. He has two kids just like my mom. That's about it."

"Wow, makes for a big family." Joe, now with nothing left to throw, rested his arm on his good knee.

"Not really. I don't think my half brother or sisters have even met. My parents were real young when they had me . . . I wasn't exactly planned." Finny, like Joe, picked up a pebble and threw it. As much as she'd thought about her parents and the divorce, she'd never talked about it to anyone. She didn't have close friends at school and she spent most of her time at the barn where she wasn't completely accepted by the other girls her age.

"They got married thinking it was the right thing to do." Finny gave a pained chuckle with that statement. "I didn't know it, but they were real unhappy, at least my dad was." Finny looked at Joe who was looking back, listening.

"Anyway, they're both remarried with young kids, perfect families, everybody's happy. Then there's me, the fifth wheel everywhere I go."

"You don't feel like you're a part of a family?"

"Not so much. With my dad, I went through long periods of not seeing him. That about did me in when I was a kid. He used to call me the sunshine of his life, you know from the Stevie Wonder song? He'd sing me that verse to wake me up in the morning." Finny had to stop. Her eyes burned and tears came before she could stop them.

Joe, surprised by the sudden emotion, didn't know what to do. He wanted to put his arm around her shoulder, comfort her like his mother used to do when he was little, but he didn't know if it was the right thing to do when you're not little anymore.

"I'm sorry, I know your dad's still around and all, but him being gone like that . . . I could see it hurtin' bad like someone died."

"You know, Joe, that's exactly what it feels like. I'm sorry, you really did lose your parents and nothing could be worse. But it's like our whole family just died. Crap, I don't know what I'm saying." Finny buried her face in her hands. Joe felt helpless. He thought Finny would keep crying but she didn't. After a deep breath she went silent behind her hands.

"Hey, Finny, do you want to hear the Legend of the Cherokee Rose?" Finny peeked out between her fingers. She nodded and let her hands fall to her lap.

"My grandpa told me this when I was a little kid. He was full-blood Cherokee, so I know it's true." Joe cleared his throat and then began speaking as though he were reciting from a book: "In the later half of 1838, the Cherokee People were forced to leave their homes in the East. The trail to the West was long and treacherous and many died along the way. The People's hearts were heavy with sadness and their tears mingled with the dust of the trail. The Elders, who were very wise, knew that the survival of the children depended upon the strength of the women. One evening around the campfire, the Elders called upon Heaven Dweller, *Gal v la di e hi*. They told Him of the People's suffering and their tears. They were afraid the children would not survive to rebuild the Cherokee Nation. *Gal v la di e hi* spoke to them, and said:

"To let you know how much I care, I will give you a sign. In the morning, tell the women to look back along the trail. Where their tears have fallen, I will cause to grow a plant that will have seven leaves for the seven clans of the Cherokee. Amidst the plant will be a delicate white rose with five petals. In the center of the blossom will be a pile of gold to remind the Cherokee of the white man's greed for the gold found on the Cherokee homeland. This plant will be sturdy and strong with stickers on all the stems. It will defy anything that tries to destroy it.

"The next morning the Elders told the women to look back down the trail. A plant was growing fast and covering the trail where they had walked. As the women watched, blossoms formed and slowly opened. They forgot their sadness. Like the plant, the women began to feel strong and beautiful. As the plant protected its blossoms, they knew they would have the courage and determination to protect their children who would begin a new Nation in the West.

"My grandfather told me unending strength is the trait of all great women. I believed that story 'cause my mom was so strong, not in size and muscles, but in heart, and Finny, I think you're like that too."

Finny was stunned into silence. She'd never been spoken to so beautifully. Joe's face was open and honest. She felt weak just looking at him. He was waiting for her to say something. Finny knew this, but her head and her heart were reeling.

"Three hundred seventy-five," rang out from the speaker.

"Hey, that's my number . . . only three hours, can you believe it?"

"No . . . I can't." Finny stood and offered Joe her hand to help him up. He stretched his leg and they made their way inside.

"Joe McCoy," the nurse from earlier yelled to the crowd.

"Right here." Finny waved to the nurse who then motioned them over.

"Okay, son, right this way. Miss, this could take a while."

"Okay, good luck, Joe." Finny wanted to hug him so badly but stood and waved instead. Joe gave her a quick smile before disappearing down the hall.

There were some seats available now, but the smell

was sickening, so she went back outside to their spot. She sat by the tree and thought of Cherokee women and roses.

"Finny, wake up." She struggled to consciousness; the light had changed and shadows now surrounded her. Finally awake, Finny got to her feet. Joe stood in front of her with a huge brace on his leg and crutches under both arms. She took a quick glance at her watch. It was long after four.

"So is it broken?"

"Yep."

"Ugh! That's not a cast though, it's just a brace."

"Yeah, because it's my kneecap. I have to wear the brace for six weeks and I'm not supposed to walk on it."

"Six weeks, that's like forever!"

"I know. I gotta get a job and a place to live. I hope I can with this." Joe motioned toward the brace.

"No, you can't strain it. We can keep doing what we're doing for six more weeks."

"You can't keep taking care of me. I gotta get a job."

"Joe, you're a fifteen-year-old with no ID and a broken leg. Who's going to hire you?"

Joe let out a groan and closed his eyes. "I don't know, someone stupid?"

Finny laughed out loud. "Come on, we gotta get to the bus stop before it's too late."

"Okay, lead the way."

"You know, you move a lot faster with the crutches. Does it still hurt?"

"Not so much now." Finny and Joe made it to the stop with only moments to spare. The bus pulled up and they hurried on board hoping for the very back so Joe could stretch out his leg. They got what they wanted and settled in for the long ride.

"Thanks again, Finny."

She smiled. She wanted to reach over and hold his hand. It'd probably feel right, but she couldn't make herself do it.

"No problem, Joe."

Chapter Five

———

"LOOK, HIS HEAD IS UP AND ALL HIS FOOD IS gone." Sky nickered loudly when he saw Finny. Joe caught up to her as she was putting the halter on the horse.

"How's the ringworm?"

"About gone."

Finny led Sky from his quarantine corral to the grooming area next to it. He danced around and fidgeted before settling down to get brushed. Finny began with the currycomb. She rubbed the dead and sunscorched hair off.

"It hasn't even been two weeks and look at the difference. You did a great job on his tail."

"Thanks, but look at his feet. They're gonna need shoes."

"I gotta save a little more money."

"I know how to shoe. I need tools, but I can do it."

"You can? Are you serious? Vel has tools but no shoes. Can you trim?"

"Yep, I sure can, and he needs it bad. That's a nasty toe crack." Finny ran to the shed and got the farrier tools.

"I can't hold his leg right because of the brace. Can you hold it up?"

"Of course!"

Twenty minutes later Sky's feet looked remarkably better. Joe trimmed with skill and ease; he balanced the hoof perfectly. Finny knew there was an art to it; you had to have an instinct and an eye for correctness. Joe had it, no question.

"You're amazing. How did you learn?"

"Being around horses and farriers who were willing to teach me."

"I bet once your leg gets better you could make good money shoeing."

"I can ride and train, too. Well, I could anyway."

"Your leg will get better. You will again. I can't wait to see you ride. I bet you're great."

Joe gave a half smile, then his eyes got far away. Finny recognized this look now. It was thinking about his past that put him there. She also knew it'd be a while before he was upbeat again.

"I want to see if he knows how to lunge. Will you come with me?"

Joe nodded and grabbed his crutches. Finny led Sky, who danced energetically at the end of the line, all the way to the arena. Once in the ring Finny let out some slack and tried to get the horse to move around her in a circle. Sky kept turning to face her instead.

"You have to drive more from the hindquarters, that'll send him forward."

Finny moved back and lined up with Sky's hipbone. That was all it took; he moved forward and around her in a brisk walk.

"Joe, that totally worked." Sky walked with a spring in his step. He was feeling better as well as looking better.

"Try a trot."

Finny gave Sky a cluck and he stepped instantly into a trot.

"He knows how to lunge!" Finny said. "This is so great!"

"That'll make breakin' him a lot easier."

"I can't wait. How long till you think we should try?"

"Well," Joe said, "let's wait another couple weeks before putting the saddle and bridle on. If he gets some fat over his bones the saddle won't rub sores."

"Good thinking. Joe, look at him move. His feet aren't even healed and look how big his step is."

"He does look like he's gonna have a big stride."

"Wouldn't it be amazing if he could jump? It'd be a dream come true for me."

"I hope he can, Finny, I really do."

After five minutes Sky got tired and broke to a walk. Finny let him cool before taking him to graze next to the arena. Joe came with her and sat on a big rock. He rested the crutches against it.

"How's your leg?"

"It doesn't hurt. It itches under the brace though."

"Four more weeks, then it's off and you'll be able to walk and ride pain free. Once your leg is better, I think it'll be time to tell Vel. I'm hoping you'll trust her by then. Besides, she'd know how to find you a job."

"I don't know, Finny. I've never had much luck trusting adults. She'd feel it was her duty to tell the police or somebody that a minor just appeared out of nowhere."

"Maybe you're right. So, Joe, where *did* you appear from?"

"That's kind of a hard question to answer."

"You know you can trust me."

"I know."

"But if you don't want to say, it's okay."

"It's not that. . . . It's just I've been living all over the country the last few years, but I grew up in Horse Mountain, Montana."

"Wow, I like the sound of that. I never heard of Horse Mountain, Montana."

"That's what the Indians called it. It's probably

named something else on maps. We were right outside Sweetgrass on the Canadian border."

"It must be beautiful up there."

"It was. Heaven on earth . . . When I picture my parents in heaven, I picture Horse Mountain."

"I'll bet heaven does look like that, Joe."

"My uncle says there's no heaven and when we die we just go to dirt, but I think he's wrong."

"Your uncle is wrong. I see little pieces of heaven every day."

"Where?" Joe locked his gaze on her. Finny was caught off guard by his sudden intensity.

"You're gonna think I'm nuts."

"No I won't."

"Little everyday things . . . Sky's nicker when he sees me. The rain when it cools you down just right. When I walk through a forest so thick I can't see the sky, but streaks of gold sunshine cut through the leaves and light up the ground. I always look up into the gold light knowing it will blind me, but I don't care. It's like a pathway to heaven."

"You sound so sure."

"I am."

Joe smiled, a big smile that said, *If you have hope, I can too.*

"Joe! Joe, are you over there?" Elsa's voice cut

through the air, startling them both. She was at the fence line at the edge of Silver Spur property.

"There you are," Elsa said as she slipped through the fence.

"What are you doing here, Elsa?" Finny asked, trying not to show her annoyance. Elsa had surely never stepped foot on Azure Hills before.

"Oh, hello, Finny. Didn't see you."

"Joe, I have a job for you if you still need one."

"Yes, I do. What? Where?"

"My groom needs help. So you'd work for me helping with my horses."

"Elsa, you only have four horses. Since when does that require two grooms?"

"Since I decided it did. What do you say, Joe, ten bucks an hour?"

"Yes . . . Oh, I'm on crutches for four more weeks. Is that a problem?"

"No, don't worry. Whatever you can't do, Omar will. Follow me. I'll show you what needs to be done." Finny stopped him with a touch to his arm. Joe looked at her; his face said it all—he wanted the job, he needed the job.

"So, I'll meet you back here in an hour?" Finny said. Joe nodded.

"No, that won't work. I'll take him home when we're done. Ready to go, Joe?"

"Yes. I guess I'll see you later, Finny." Joe slid through the fence and pulled the crutches after him. He gave Finny a wave, then turned and followed Elsa toward the Silver Spur barn.

Finny tried to keep her thoughts light but it felt like the air had turned to mud. Joe wasn't her boyfriend, she reminded herself as she put Sky in his corral. He was just a friend. Sky anxiously weaved back and forth waiting for his hay. He was getting more energetic every day. Finny watched him eat for a moment before she went to feed the rest of the horses. She was tossing a flake of hay to Roman, a small bay Arabian in the last stall, when she realized that Joe was more than a friend; he was a best friend. When he was around she felt right and fine and good enough and pretty enough, or at least being pretty enough didn't matter. Maybe it was more than friendship. The thought of him with Elsa burned a hole in her gut. Elsa always got what she wanted and Finny knew, without a doubt, she wanted Joe.

Depressed, Finny finished up feeding the rest of the horses, then headed for the end of the drive. Her mom would be there to pick her up and always got mad if Finny was late, even though she, herself, was frequently late . . . or early. Either way, her mom was always cranky about it. Between the twins, her new social circle, and redecorating the house, her mom was busy. The horse stuff was at the other end of town, always out of the way. Her mom thought it was bad enough that Finny worked at Silver Spur, but when Finny told her she had started helping out with the horses at Azure Hills her mother simply shook her head. Finny hadn't yet told her mom about Sky. She figured she'd ease into the truth in small stages.

It was now 7:20 AM. Her mom was twenty minutes late. Finny sat on the big boulder next to the Azure Hills sign and checked her watch again. She looked toward the Silver Spur barn, then rolled her eyes and shook her head, wondering how Elsa had talked her dad into another groom.

Just then she spotted Elsa's car driving down the Silver Spur drive. She didn't want to be seen just sitting here. Maybe Joe would ask Elsa to stop and give her a ride. Finny laughed to herself. Elsa would do it in an effort to not look so mean. Finny could just make out the two occupants. Elsa got to the road. Finny readied herself for whatever would happen when she passed. Elsa turned the other way. The wrong way if she were taking Joe to the trailer park. Finny jumped off the rock and

watched as the car disappeared in the distance. She felt
her eyes go hot. Where were they going? Why were they
going somewhere other than home? Finny paced back
and forth and fought back tears. *Get a grip*, she told
herself. She looked at her watch—7:30. Her mom was
half an hour late and it was almost dark. Finny made
her way back down the driveway to use Vel's phone.

"Hey, Mom, are you coming?"

"Of course, lost track of the time. I'll be there soon."

"Okay, I'll be at the Azure Hills sign."

She left the house and walked down the drive. Once
at the boulder she got comfortable, let out a sigh, and
rested her head in her crossed arms. It was bad enough
feeling like the fifth wheel. She hated the constant proof.

At seven the next morning Finny was at the door to
the trailer. She knocked softly but Joe, being a sound
sleeper, typically didn't answer. Finny used her key and
opened the door. The trailer was hot and stuffy from
not having the windows opened last night. They weren't
opened because no one had slept there. Finny checked
all the rooms. No Joe and the food hadn't been touched.
He had never come home. Before she knew it tears were
streaming down her face. Finny wiped them away with
the back of her hand and left the trailer, locking the

door behind her. She'd been walking to the trailer each morning so that she could walk with Joe to the barn, since that's all he could do. Now she wished she had her bike. She'd make it to Azure Hills in fifteen minutes instead of thirty.

In the short time she'd known Joe, Finny had found him to be a set-in-his-ways kind of person. She'd thought for sure he'd come back. Maybe Elsa had a better place for him to live. Maybe he really got to like her and didn't want to come back. Finny's thoughts tortured her throughout the entire walk. She arrived at Azure Hills and walked down the drive.

Still teary, Finny dried her eyes for what she hoped was the last time. She'd focus on her horse. That's what mattered—they never let you down. A sweet nicker of a hello was as warm as any hug.

Rounding the corner of the barn, Finny spotted Joe propped up against Sky's stall. He was wrapped in a horse blanket, sound asleep. Tears came back full force. Seeing him there, knowing he wasn't with Elsa, flooded her with relief and pure joy. Finny gave herself a moment to get her emotions under control. She didn't get it—she was like a nut around him and quickly turning into her most dreaded stereotype.

"Joe." She shook his shoulder.

"Hey, Finny," Joe said first thing.

"Did you sleep here all night?"

"Yeah, it was pretty late by the time I got here and my leg was hurtin'."

"What happened with Elsa?"

"Not really sure." Joe rubbed his head, grabbed his crutches, and stood. "She shows me her horses, tells me about them, how much they cost, and how much she'd won, but not a word about what she wants me to do no matter how many times I asked."

"Oh. Where did you guys go? I saw you drive off."

Joe heaved out a sigh. "Shopping. She said she'd take me back after making a quick stop. This stop was a store and two of the girls from the barn were waiting there."

"Shopping? For what?"

"Clothes . . . for me." Joe rolled his eyes. "She said she wanted her groom to look first rate."

"Oh, wow . . . what did you say?"

"That I don't want her buying me clothes. The three of them were all gigglin' and carryin' on. I was pretty aggravated by then and just wanted to go back."

"I'm surprised she did that. Could be she was trying to be nice?"

"I don't think so . . . I'm not sure what it was. She reminded me of my uncle. What he'd do when he was trying to con someone. He'd be all nice—and my uncle ain't nice. He'd talk big and say all the right things. It worked, too. People believed him . . . it always worked."

"You think she was doing that?"

"Know she was. I just don't know why. I asked her to bring me back but it was like talkin' to bricks. I didn't know where I was so I just rode it out. Finally she got mad and brought me back here. I don't think I have a job now," Joe said the last part with a laugh.

"What made her mad?"

"I refused to try on clothes."

"Oh, man, Elsa isn't used to not getting her way." Finny had to hold back a laugh. "You survived her wrath, though."

"Barely," Joe said with mock seriousness.

Finny burst out laughing. "Let's see if Vel has something for breakfast." Finny and Joe walked up the back stairs to Vel's porch and knocked on the door. A just-awakened Vel answered.

"Oh, sorry, did we wake you?"

"Yeah, but it's okay; it was time. What's up?"

"You know when you said anytime we were hungry to come knock on your door?"

"I sure do. Come on in."

"Thanks, Vel. We're hoping to get an early start so we can get everything done before it gets too hot."

"Sounds smart to me. How do you guys feel about pancakes with bacon and eggs?"

"Sounds like heaven!"

Vel got all the ingredients out of the cabinets and prepared the batter for the pancakes. "Finny, will you grab the bacon?"

"You bet."

"Joe, do you know how to scramble eggs?"

Joe shook his head. Finny opened the package of bacon and put several strips on a pan. Finny glanced over at Joe. He was standing in the corner, not speaking and not making eye contact.

"Do you want to learn how to make scrambled eggs?" Vel asked. When Joe didn't answer Finny stepped in.

"Sure he does!" Joe grimaced at Finny, then went to stand next to Vel.

"Okay, Joe, break these eggs and put them in this bowl."

Joe did as instructed.

"Careful not to get the shells in."

Joe was more careful and broke the rest shell-free.

"Perfect. Now we add a little milk, a dash of salt and pepper, and use this for the eggs." Vel handed Joe something he'd never seen before. He looked to Finny and held it up. She motioned with her hand how to use the whisk and Joe repeated it to stir the eggs.

"Perfect. Next we turn the heat on under the pan, put in a little butter. Try to whip them enough to get air in them so they're fluffy."

Joe nodded and doubled his efforts.

"How's the bacon coming, Finny?"

"Getting there." While letting the food slowly cook, Finny and Vel set the table. Joe diligently stood over the eggs to make sure they didn't burn.

"Good job, Joe. They look ready. Turn off the heat and put them on the plates."

"Perfect timing—my bacon is done."

"I'll grab some O.J. and the pancakes. Kids, go ahead, sit and eat." All three crammed around the small table that sat against the window overlooking the horses. Vel's house was a modest three-bedroom with two baths. Built years ago, its age was obvious, but Vel kept things tidy and clean.

"So what do you kids have planned for today?"

"We'll feed, muck, medicate, and turn out, then I'll go to Silver Spur to work."

Vel noticed Joe had eaten everything in front of him. "I'll go make some more eggs and bacon." Finny, still working on hers, thanked Vel.

"How's the leg?" Vel nodded toward Joe's brace. He shrugged. Vel scrambled up more eggs and put them on Joe's plate.

"Thank you."

"So you do speak."

"Yes, ma'am."

Vel gave Joe a smile and put the pan in the sink. She saw Joe's crutches and noted the free clinic's sticker. Puzzle pieces began to fall into place.

"Joe, I'm guessing you're a runaway."

Joe half choked on his eggs. After coughing, sputtering, and a slap on the back from Finny he could breathe again. Joe shot Finny a look.

"What? I didn't say anything."

"She didn't, Joe. I'm sorry to startle you, but it makes sense. The first day I saw you, you had bruises on your face and a split lip on top of older fading bruises."

Finny looked at Joe with raised eyebrows. She hadn't noticed older bruises. Joe pushed his food around on his plate but made no comment.

"You're staying in Finny's old trailer and your clothes are always the same, not to mention old and worn out."

"Are you going to call the police?" Joe asked without taking his eyes from his food.

"I was sixteen when I left home. I left for what I'm guessing is the same reason you did, so no, I'm not calling anybody."

Chapter Six

Four weeks of horse ownership and Finny felt Sky was coming along right on track. No longer in quarantine, Sky now had a choice stall in the barn. Finny took him to the arena. Once there she undid the lead and instantly Sky spun away, blasting off at a gallop.

"Finny," Joe said, "he shouldn't pull away like that. You should use a stud chain. He needs to respect you."

"He's never done that before." Joe and Finny watched as Sky raced around the arena bucking and playing.

"Wow, look at him go," Finny said, breathless.

"Do you know how much he was handled?" Joe asked, leaning on his crutches.

"No idea." Sky continued to tear around the ring.

"Well, he's feeling better," Joe said. "Has energy now that he's gained some weight."

"I guess I'll go catch him."

"Wait a few minutes, let him get all this steam out of his system."

For the next twenty minutes the kids watched Sky prance and dance around, his movements fluid and beautiful.

"I think it's safe now."

Finny nodded and went into the arena. When Sky saw her approach he trotted to her.

"Joe, did you see that? He came to me!"

"Yes," Joe said with worry.

Finny clipped on the lead and brought Sky to the grooming area. He danced on the end of the line but soon settled to be groomed.

"Look at him, his coat is really starting to shine and his ribs are disappearing," Joe said with a pat on Sky's hip.

Finny smiled and curried away. Joe got comfortable on a chair and brushed out Sky's now long, luxurious, knot-free tail. After two minutes the horse began to move around and paw the ground hard with his hoof. Joe knew this, too, was a bad sign.

"Why is he pawing? Do you think he's sick?"

"No, I think he's irritated because he's bored. Let's go lunge him." Joe grabbed his crutches and the lunge line. He handed it to Finny. She led Sky back to the arena and began to let out the line so he could trot around her. Sky trotted one circle around Finny and then bolted, burning the rope out of her hand. Finny gasped and grabbed her injured palm. Sky, like a maniac, ran around the ring full speed trailing the lunge line behind him.

"Get out of there!" Joe yelled.

"I gotta stop him, he'll tangle the line around his leg. He'll get hurt!"

"You can't stop him. Come out now!"

Finny waited for a break, and when Sky skidded to a stop at the railing, she dashed out of the arena. She turned back and watched him.

"Why is he acting so crazy?"

"I'm not so sure you're gonna like my answer."

"Tell me."

"I think he's completely wild. I don't think he's been handled enough. What looked like a calm, docile horse was a sick, weak one."

The teens continued to watch as Sky tore up the arena. When he finally slowed to a trot Finny grabbed a pair of gloves, went back in, and picked up the end of the lunge line.

"Try now to lunge him. Get him to move away from you and then stop. Do that like three times. See if he's at least willing to listen a little."

Finny clucked; Sky went forward and tried to pull away. It took all her strength not to lose him again.

"I can't control him, Joe."

"Try one more time—go then stop. When you stop pull him toward you. Talk to him."

"Come on, Sky, walk forward," she made a clucking sound. Sky walked on.

"Now, firm voice, tell him *whoa* and pull him toward you." Joe said.

"Whoa, Sky," Finny said in a loud deep voice. With all her might, Finny pulled. Sky turned and stopped.

"It worked!"

"Doesn't mean he'll stay there. Talk to him and bring him out now; let's get him put away." Using both hands Finny led the horse back to his stall.

"I'm sorry, Finny. I feel so useless with my bum leg. As soon as I'm better, I'll help handle him."

"Don't worry, you've already been hurt once by a horse. I'll be fine."

"A horse didn't . . ." Joe stopped midsentence. He looked at Finny, saw her expression, and wished he could take back what he'd said. Finny put Sky away, then hosed off her still-burning palm at the wash rack just outside the barn.

"How's your hand?" Joe asked. He felt terrible being caught in a lie to someone he liked so much, whose trust he had earned. Joe knew Finny was upset and couldn't blame her. She attended to her hand, ignoring him.

Joe sat on the bench at the end of the barn aisle. "I raced horses. Not the races you'd see on TV—these were illegal, back-alley races that weren't even on a track. They happen after the rodeos close and the crowds are gone. No rules or law applied, just a lot of money to be made if you won. My uncle . . ." Joe closed his eyes, took a breath, and began again. "Losing wasn't an option. I liked to win, and I did. Enough that the other riders started to threaten me. I thought they were just trying to psyche me out. You know, shake my confidence." Joe paused for a moment and glanced over at Finny. He took off his hat and rubbed his forehead. "I was wrong. I got jumped and beat on. The last thing I remember was this man standing over me holding a board in his hand; he said my racing days were over. Then my knee exploded. I'm sorry I lied to you, Finny. I won't ever lie to you again."

Finny sat by Joe's side, took his hand, and held it. She felt like throwing up. She wished she knew what to say or do, but sitting with him, staying by his side, holding his hand seemed right, so that's what she did.

Chapter Seven

"TWO HUNDRED AND FIFTY POUNDS IN FIVE weeks." Finny took the measuring tape from around Sky's midsection. "Can you believe he's gained that much?"

"Yes," Vel said. "He's unrecognizable from the horse you brought in here." She gave Sky a rub on his muzzle and admired his now shiny mahogany coat that glistened with dapples and good health.

"No more bald spots, and look at his tail—ever seen one so full and thick?"

Vel gave a chuckle at how proud Finny was about her horse. And she should be; he was beautiful.

"I see champion in him, Vel, I know it's there."

"I hope so, honey, I really do." Vel gave Sky a pat, then headed off to work.

Joe came around the corner sporting a crutch under one arm and a saddle, pad, and girth draped over the other.

"Let's try the saddle today. Since we can lunge him now with control, it's time."

"Where's your other crutch?"

"By the house. I get around faster on one."

"You only have one more week. Don't mess with your knee now!"

"I'm not, I promise." Joe placed the tack on a rail next to the crosstie. "Go lunge him, get his energy down, and then we'll put the saddle on."

Now using a lead line with a section of chain over his nose for added control, Finny led Sky to the arena. He danced at her side. She worked on his manners, insisting he walk next to her, not in front or back and not banging into her every other step. At 17.2 hands and thirteen hundred pounds, he was not fun to bump into.

Finny and Joe had found that Sky was willing to learn, but his attention span was extremely short.

Out in the arena Finny slowly let out slack in the lunge line. Sky had taken to bolting when lunged and they'd worked long and hard to get him to behave like a gentleman. So far so good. Sky was walking. Finny gave a cluck and Sky bounded off at a trot. He was a fancy mover; he had the kind of motion judges like to see in the show ring. Muscle that sprang from nowhere rippled under his shiny coat and his luxurious tail fluttered in the breeze. Finny could spend the rest of her life just watching her beautiful horse and have no regrets.

"Look at him go. His stride is huge!" Joe said, leaning on his crutch, watching Sky trot by.

"They want big strides in jumping horses. I sure hope he can jump."

"I don't have much experience with jumpers, but he looks like he could do anything," Joe said.

Finny brought Sky back down to a walk and led him toward the gate.

"We should saddle him in here," Joe said. "If he doesn't like it we'll have more room to handle him."

"I'll go grab the saddle."

Once Finny was gone Joe whispered into Sky's ear. "You be a good boy, Sky; make Finny happy. She's the sweetest person on earth and the best owner you'll ever have, so behave." Joe gave Sky a pat just as Finny rounded the corner with the saddle, minus its stirrups. He'd get used to the saddle first before being introduced to stirrups banging his sides.

"Okay, rub him with the saddle pad first, all over his body. With as much as he's been groomed it shouldn't bother him." Joe was right—Sky didn't flinch. After a few moments he looked bored.

"Okay, lay it in place then do the same with the saddle."

Finny did as instructed and two minutes later Sky stood quietly with a saddle on his back for the first time in his life.

"Can you believe it? He has a saddle on!"

"That was the easy part. Now the girth. Rub his belly where the girth is going to touch."

Finny did and Sky moved around a bit but soon settled down.

"Okay, put the girth on loose."

"Like this?"

"Yep, you got it. Now walk a few steps."

Sky walked along quietly.

"Okay, now tighten it just enough for him to feel it, then walk some more."

Again, Finny did as she was told and Sky behaved like a gentleman.

"He's so perfect, look at him."

"Finny, so far there's no pressure. He may act up once he feels some, so be careful. Go ahead and tighten it one more time."

Finny did and Sky flicked his ears back and forth and swished his tail hard.

"I don't think he likes it."

"He's not used to it. Give him some time. Walk him again."

"Is it too tight?"

"No, he just feels it now. Keep walking."

Finny moved forward and Sky began to dance next to her.

"Let him loose. Give him time to deal with it on his own." Joe could sense the horse was going to act up. Finny unhooked the lead and got out through the gate of the arena just in time. Sky exploded away and let out the biggest buck Finny had ever seen. Within moments he was tearing around the arena like a rodeo bronc. The saddle stayed snugly where it belonged.

For five solid minutes Sky bucked, ran, and reared but nothing dislodged the saddle.

"He looks so mad. We need to stop him so we can get it off," Finny said, wringing her hands with worry.

"No, let him deal. It's not hurting him. What you said is right—he's mad."

"Is that normal for a horse to get so mad?"

"Not really, but Sky being twelve, growin' up with people instead of other horses, makes him a little harder to understand."

Sky, finally tired from running, stopped and reached around to bite the hated saddle.

"Have you ever seen a horse do that, Joe?"

"Bite at a saddle? No, never."

Talking in soothing tones, Finny went to Sky, clipped on his lead, and removed the saddle. Once it was off all was forgiven and Sky was happy. Finny walked him out of the arena, then turned him out in the pasture to graze.

"I still say today was a milestone."

"It was." Joe smiled and leaned on the fence. He adjusted his immobilizer to make it more comfortable.

"How's the leg? A few more days and that will come off. I bet you can't wait."

"I'm so ready. The last couple of weeks it hasn't hurt or anything. I just want to ride again."

"I can't wait to see you ride. I bet you're awesome."

"You know who was great? My dad. He'd gentle the rankest horse in a day. My mom used to say he was half cowboy, half magician." Finny saw Joe's face turn from happy to slack, breaking her heart.

"I'm sorry, Joe."

He gave a half smile, then stood up. "I'm gonna start on the stalls. How long will you be at Silver Spur?"

"Most of the day. Are you sure you're okay doing everything here?"

"Oh, yeah. I've gotten good at moving around with this thing." Joe tapped his brace.

"Okay, I'll be back as soon as I can." Finny hated to leave but she had to. She slid though the fence and waved good-bye.

The feed store truck was pulling up Silver Spur's

long driveway. Finny hurried so she could help Dale unload the bags of feed into the feed room. She also knew he'd be distracted because most of the girls at the barn had a crush on him. Finny wasn't surprised when Olivia and Josie were already by the feed room waiting. Dale backed the truck up to the door and hopped out. He was sixteen, tall, blond, and handsome. His feed store job and the high school football team kept him muscle-bound and fit.

"Hello," Dale said to the gathering group of girls.

"Hi, Dale," Josie said. "What'd you bring?"

Finny did her best not to smile. Josie's crush was glaringly obvious.

"Grain, grain, and more grain," Dale said, hefting two bags at once over his shoulders. Finny could only handle one fifty-pound bag at a time. Dale climbed the stairs and dumped the bags on the floor of the feed room.

"Thanks," he said to Finny as she passed by with a bag.

"So you go to Chesterfield High, right?" Olivia asked.

"I do." He answered politely but had to keep moving. There were several deliveries to do.

"I go to Collinwood Prep."

"Do you?" Dale stated. Again, polite and no doubt

used to twelve-year-old barn girls with crushes. Finny tried not to laugh. Chesterfield was where she attended school. Elsa and her buddies called it the "last chance school for losers."

Finny began to pour the bags of grain into the metal feed containers. If they left the grain in the paper bags, the mice would tear them open to feast.

By bag ten she was getting tired and Dale kept bringing more. Carl was nowhere to be seen, so Finny knew she had to be the one to get this done.

When Dale dropped the last bag he hesitated, then began opening bags and helping Finny pour them into the feed bins.

"It's okay, I know you're busy. I got this."

"It's no problem." Josie and Olivia were soon joined by Audrey, Clara, and Raine. They all watched Finny and Dale work while peppering Dale with questions. He worked fast and had no problem lifting the heavy bags or answering the girls' endless questions with good humor. With Dale's help all the grain was stored in less than fifteen minutes.

"Have a good day, ladies." Dale waved and smiled before hustling to his truck.

"Thank you!" Finny yelled after him. Josie had a dreamy look on her face as she grabbed Olivia's arm and walked away.

"What do you think, Clara, Dale cuter than Finny's non-boyfriend?" Audrey said, not at all trying to hide her mocking tone.

"Hard to say. No-bo Joe was pretty sweet."

"No-bo Joe! Clara, that's classic."

Finny had to push past them to get out of the feed room. As much as she wanted to say something back, she knew better and wasn't going to jeopardize her ability to work there.

Finny took her job list from her pocket. Again it was daunting. She needed to groom, wrap, and turn out all the horses that weren't getting training rides today. That was sixteen. Finny picked up a jog. That was only one chore out of twenty-five.

Vel Moore pulled into her drive and parked behind her house. She spotted Joe with her two retired horses, Max and Stella, in the wash rack. He was bathing Stella and Max was drying in the sun, his coat now sparkling white.

"This is a nice surprise." Joe jumped when she spoke.

"Sorry, Joe, didn't mean to sneak up on you."

"Hope you don't mind. I was just done cleanin' and all. I figured it'd be okay to bathe 'em."

"Of course. I've been so busy at work I haven't had the time."

"I'm happy to take care of them. All of 'em, if you want."

"Whatever you can do is great. And Joe, please help yourself to the food in the fridge. I'm tight on money at the moment, but the least I could do is feed you. Oh, and Finny says you can trim and shoe. I could pay you for that. The farrier I got now is retiring."

"Thank you, ma'am . . . Sorry, Vel." She gave him a smile. Getting him to remember to call her Vel was taking a while, but he was getting there.

"I'm going to make us both some lunch. Come in when you're done." Vel turned away before Joe could decline her offer. She knew he had to be hungry, but she also knew he wasn't comfortable around her and she was hoping to change that.

By five o'clock Joe was getting worried about Finny. He went to the fence line and spotted her heading his way through the trees. She looked exhausted.

"What are they doing to you over there?" he asked as Finny slipped through the fence.

"Pretty much all of my work and Carl's. I swear I never see him anymore."

"Anything here left to be done?" Finny asked, still ready to work if needed.

"No, all done. I just fed, too."

"Ready to head back to the trailer then?"

"You bet. I wish Vel was here to give us a ride. You look dead."

Finny smiled and shrugged her shoulders. "No biggie. I just want to say hi to Sky before we head off." Seeing her horse clean and happy re-energized Finny. She filled Joe in on her day at Silver Spur as they walked to the trailer.

When they arrived at the mobile home, a brand new "For Sale" sign was staked out on the lawn.

"Oh no! What if my mom went inside or around back? I'm so dead."

"No, you're not. I make sure no one can tell anyone's been here before I leave. And I wanted to surprise you, but I fixed the backyard."

"How'd you do that?"

"Tools in the carport. Two big pieces of siding, too. Everything's fixed, you'd never know," Joe said proudly.

"Joe, you are a life saver, thank you!" Finny jumped up and grabbed him in a hug. Joe's whole body locked tight. Finny quickly let go. Trying to think of anything to break the sudden awkwardness, she stammered, "I, uh . . . bet Vel would let you stay with her if you can't stay here and she can help you enroll at the high school."

"High school? I haven't been to school since I was eleven."

"You're kidding. What did you do? How did you learn stuff?"

"Learned all kinds of things. How to ride, break, rope, work cattle, tend sheep, shoe horses, mend fences. I can heal a horse that's sick, or hurt. I can fix cars, trucks, tractors, anything with a motor. I know most of the drivelines through the country and how and when to run them. I can hunt, fish, and track a missing animal for miles if we lose one. I know how to survive the desert in the summer and the mountains in the winter. I watched my uncle and how he handled his business. So I know how to lie, cheat, and steal if I had a mind to."

"Wow . . . that's more than I could ever do."

Joe laughed. "I don't know if those things will get me anywhere these days. A lot of the old-timers I used to know said the world changed and there's no going back. Cowboys will soon be extinct like the dinosaurs."

"I hope that's not true."

"If I had my wish, I'd just work with horses. Gotta figure out how to get paid to do it."

"Me, too, Joe. I want to be a trainer and teach people to ride and go to horse shows just like Jeff next door."

"He any good?"

"I think so. He wins a lot. He costs a lot."

Joe nodded and sat on the couch. He stretched out his right leg and eased back into the cushions. Finny glanced at her watch. She wanted to hang with Joe but knew she had to get home. She turned and looked at him, wondering how he felt. Wondering if he wanted her to stay or if it mattered either way. She wished he were a little easier to read.

"I'm going to head for home."

"Okay."

Finny searched his face for signs he wanted her to stay. There were none.

"Do you get bored here all by yourself with no TV or anything?"

"Bored? No, I like it here. It's peaceful."

"That's good then. I'll see you tomorrow."

"See you tomorrow." Joe stood when Finny got up to leave. He waved, and then closed the door. Finny made her way back to her house. Maybe tomorrow she'd ask how he felt about things. If he asked, *What things?* she'd just say, *I don't know. Things.*

When Finny walked into her house her mom was moving suitcases out of the garage and into the hallway.

"Are you going on a vacation?"

"Oh, hi, Finny. Yes, next weekend Steven and I are taking the girls to Magical Beginnings. They've been dying to go. So you'll be staying with your dad."

"Is that like Disneyland for little kids?"

"You could say that."

"That's not Dad's normal weekend."

"I know, but he said it was okay."

"Hey Mom . . ."

"Yes?" Finny was getting up the nerve to ask why, when there were trips to take, she was always sent to the other parent and never included. She knew her mom would say, well this is for little kids and you'd be bored. She knew that because that's what her father said when she asked him. Finny wanted to ask if maybe they could do something that the whole family could do together, just once so she didn't feel so unimportant, but she didn't, because it would be unbearable hearing that she was a mistake and a burden to them now that they had the families they really wanted.

"I hope you all have fun."

"Thanks, sweetheart."

Finny went upstairs to her room, lay on her bed, and let her mind wander. She gazed around her bedroom, then got up and went to the bathroom. Once there, she looked into the mirror and tapped it lightly just to feel how solid it was. Her mind went back to Joe. She wondered if he thought she was pretty. Or if, once out of sight, he thought about her at all.

Finny pulled her hair back, then up. She let it drop

and stared at her face. Joe was handsome. He sure didn't act it, though. Maybe it didn't matter to him . . . maybe he didn't know. Could be if you don't have people telling you you're handsome or pretty, you don't know.

Next weekend was the last summer weekend before school started. Finny sighed, left the bathroom, and flopped back down on her bed. She didn't want to waste her last weekend with her dad who acted like a stranger or a stepmother who seemed to confuse a visiting daughter with a maid/babysitter.

A fat warm tear rolled down Finny's cheek. Caught by surprise, she wiped it away. She was tired of being fourteen.

Finny closed her eyes and thought of Sky and what to do next. He was coming along . . . fine. As soon as Joe was off his crutches they'd break him to ride. Finny knew without Joe's help she'd have been lost. She had only ever ridden very broke, well-trained show horses. Even the sour ones like Tank had years of experience, and they were nothing like her giant, more dog-than-horse-acting equine.

Finny rolled over and got under the covers. She felt unusually tired and wished she were still with Joe. She didn't know why, but everything always felt right when he was around.

Chapter Eight

JOE WOKE WHEN THE LIGHT TOUCHED HIS EYES. He had always been a rise-with-the-sun person. He sat up in bed and pulled the sheets and blankets up around him and squeezed the soft material in his hands. Having spent most of the last four years sleeping in the back of a truck or on the floor of a camper, this was paradise.

Joe pushed the blankets away and uncovered his leg. He unstrapped the immobilizer and pulled it off, then touched his knee. The doctor had said six weeks in an immobilizer might work, but he had recommended surgery. Joe feared surgery would lead to too many questions, hence too many problems. His knee felt better. It felt solid and didn't hurt when pressed on. Joe slid his leg off the bed keeping it straight. He let his knee bend slightly. To his delight there was no sudden, stabbing pain. Not wanting to push his luck, Joe put the immobilizer back on.

Allowing himself a moment of enjoyment, Joe lay back on the pillows. Six weeks since he'd slipped out of the truck and jumped into the horse trailer. It felt like a lifetime ago. Joe wondered how hard his uncle was looking for him or if he'd given up. He knew his uncle would want revenge. Would that be enough to keep him searching? Joe said a silent prayer to God and his parents never to be found.

With a weary sigh he looked around the modest trailer he didn't want to leave, then got up and made his way to the kitchen. Joe examined the contents of the refrigerator. He'd have to clean all traces of food from it when he left the trailer that morning. Thinking of all the food Finny had brought him to eat over the past six weeks made him smile. Finny, hands down, was the sweetest girl he'd ever known. Thinking of her made the smile stay. Remembering how he had reacted when she hugged him made him cringe. He had just been caught by surprise. He tried to remember the last time anyone had hugged him.

Sitting at the table, Joe poured cereal into a bowl and then milk. He always felt hungry and today was no different. He finished off the box of cereal, all the milk, and most of the bread. When living on the road, three square meals a day wasn't the norm, but the last two years having enough food not to be hungry never seemed to happen. Joe remembered his uncle complaining that he was growing too heavy, slowing the horses down. It hit him all at once—the scarce food was no accident. In a fit of anger Joe threw the empty cereal box across the room. His emotions roiled through him. He wanted to stay angry and let that fuel his resolve, but seething anger wasn't his nature and it turned into a heaviness that sapped his spirit.

Joe's thoughts went back to Finny. He was positive she was an angel sent from heaven. Why she took a chance to help him was still a mystery. Joe planned to pay her back for everything. As soon as he got a job he'd pay her for all the food she got for him. Joe knew the thing that would please her the most would be to ride her horse. He was determined to make that happen.

Still hungry, Joe finished off the rest of the bread.

Yep, Sky was the answer. If he could make Sky right, Finny's dream would come true and she deserved that.

A soft knock came from the door. Joe grabbed his crutches and met Finny as she walked into the kitchen.

"Hey, Joe." He could tell she wasn't her normal self.

"Anything wrong?"

"Just worried about where you'll stay now that we can't use the mobile home."

"If Vel won't help, I'll figure it out. Besides, I'm almost out of this thing. I'll get a job and I'll be set."

"What about school? Do you want to go back?"

Joe shrugged his shoulders. "Hadn't really thought about it. Sorta figured that part of my life was over."

"My mom says the high school years will be the best and I should enjoy them to the fullest. That's why I brought it up, but I guess it doesn't matter."

Joe sensed Finny had more to say, but didn't know how to prompt her along. He didn't understand teenagers even though he was one. "Finny, you ready to go work with Sky?"

"You bet! Maybe today he won't attack the saddle."

"That'd be nice. I think we should try the bridle too."

After a quick check to make sure everything in the home was in order and that the trailer looked unoccupied, the two began their walk.

"I turned sixteen yesterday. I can get my driver's license."

"Joe . . . yesterday was your birthday?"

"Yeah."

"Why didn't you say anything? I can't believe you didn't tell me."

"I just did."

"I mean yesterday, for crying out loud!"

"Sorry."

"Well, happy birthday! We need to do something to celebrate."

"You've done too much for me as it is. I'm just glad to be closer to eighteen."

"Well, sixteen's a milestone, a right-of-passage age. At least that's what my dad says."

"What's that mean?"

Finny laughed. "I'm not sure, but I'll be there in a little over a year. Maybe then I'll figure it out." By the time they got to Azure Hills they had their dream cars picked out.

Finny and Joe went to Sky's stall only to find it empty.

"That's weird. Maybe Vel turned him out."

Joe pointed. "He's over there grazing. I think he jumped. See the hoofprints on the ground?"

"The door is like four feet."

"It's possible. At the mustang roundups the fences are built six feet just to keep them in."

Finny made her way to Sky, speaking in soft tones.

"Come on, Sky, hold still. Let me . . ." Sky blasted off with a snort. He ran to the end of the property, then back to Finny, stopping within inches of her.

"Finny, don't let him treat you like a horse. He's playing with you. He should respect you enough not to think of you as an equal."

"What should I do?"

"Yell at him and chase him away if he runs to you again." As if on cue, Sky blasted off, digging up dirt and knocking over anything in his path. He circled the kids snorting and prancing.

"He's trying to herd us. He has no respect."

"Is that bad?"

"Yeah . . . He might not tolerate us trying to break him."

"At this point, I'd be happy just to catch him. Whoa, Sky, settle down, boy." Finny tried again to halter him. He'd stay still until she was just about to touch him, then spin away. Twenty minutes later, they were no closer.

"What are we going to do?"

"I think we need to change our strategy," Joe said. "We need to ignore him." They walked to the bench by the barn and sat.

"Don't make eye contact."

Two minutes later, having no one to play with, Sky walked to them. Neither one made a move or acknowledged his presence. Sky came almost to them and then cantered away. After a minute with no response from Finny or Joe he pawed the ground. Sky finally trotted up and bumped his head into Finny, knocking her off the bench, then stood looking down at her. Finny righted herself and grabbed a halter and slipped it on Sky's head.

"Well, we caught him."

"After he knocked you down. We've got to figure out how not to let that get any worse."

Finny led him to the crossties and grabbed the brushes. Joe got up to help her groom.

"He's hard to figure. He don't act normal," Joe said with worry.

"Normal is boring." Finny smiled, letting him know that whatever happened was fine with her. Joe went to get the saddle. Once back he laid it over the rail. Without warning Sky grabbed the saddle with his teeth and flung it across the yard. Joe froze in shock.

"Oh, geez, I guess you've never seen a horse do that either?" Finny asked, also shocked. Joe looked at her and shook his head.

"Let's take him to the ring. I'll saddle him there." Finny led Sky over, his ears pinned back, his eyes never leaving the saddle.

"Okay, Sky, behave. This doesn't hurt." Joe patted Sky's back while Finny held his halter. Sky weaved back and forth as Joe placed the saddle gently on his back. Joe patted and spoke soothing words to him as he slowly tightened the girth. Once it was on, Finny let Sky go to do what he wanted. The horse didn't move.

He just reached around, grabbed the skirt of the saddle, and ripped it off.

"Oh man, thank God we used a saddle Vel was going to throw away." Finny and Joe waited for the explosion. Sky didn't move. Like a statue he stood just trying to reach the saddle with his teeth. After five minutes of being unsuccessful Sky flung himself to the ground and rolled over the saddle repeatedly, crushing it.

Finny held her hand over her mouth, "Do you think he'll ever just deal with having a saddle?"

"Yeah, I think he will, though it's hard to believe now."

Sky suddenly shot up and began to run around the arena in earnest. Bucking, leaping, screaming. The kids did the only thing they could, sat back and watched.

"Finny, lets go to Vel's and watch him through the window. I want to see what he does when he thinks we aren't watching."

Staying as far back from the window as possible, they watched Sky. The horse instantly stopped fighting the saddle and searched for them. He paced up and down the arena fence line, then jumped over it and trotted toward the house. After grabbing a few quick bites of grass he went to the porch and sniffed it, the saddle still in place. Sky pawed at the porch, snapping a chunk of wood off.

"We gotta get out there," Joe said. "He's going to jump up on the porch."

Finny made a dash for the door. She opened it, startling Sky just enough to keep him off the steps. Like a puppy, Sky's ears were up, happy to see Finny and Joe. He ignored the saddle, which was seemingly no longer a problem.

Finny patted Sky on the nose and was able to snap on the lead.

"Let's get the bridle and try to lunge him."

Finny nodded and led Sky to the arena. Joe brought the bridle and poured honey over the bit. He gently encouraged Sky to open his mouth. Sky, enjoying the honey, didn't protest the bit. He played with it, rolling it around on his tongue, getting used to the feel.

"He doesn't seem to mind the bit."

"They usually don't. It doesn't hurt."

"It would be nice if something went easy," Finny said. Over the bridle, she placed the halter with lunge line attached and then gave a cluck to Sky to go forward. No longer full of energy after running around the ring, Sky trotted with manners on the end of the line.

"Look, Joe, saddle and a bridle, another step closer." Joe leaned on his crutch and nodded in agreement, trying to stay positive.

"Put him through his transitions, Finny."

Finny asked Sky to walk, then trot, then canter, then back to the walk and started all over again. He did everything he was supposed to.

"I think that's plenty," said Joe. "Nice how well he listened this time."

"He didn't pull on my arm or anything." Finny brought Sky back to a stop and pulled him toward her. She patted his head, then led him to his corral.

"We should put him in the stallion pen," Joe suggested. "The walls are over six feet and the doors are higher. That'll keep him in."

"Great idea. It'll give him more room, too."

They bedded Sky's new stall at the back of the barn, which opened to a large pen with a sturdy, six-foot-high fence. They gave him his grain, hay, and water and watched him eat, marveling at the amount of feed the horse consumed.

"You ready, Joe?"

"I guess," he moped.

"Vel is so cool, she'll help, I swear."

"It's just if she doesn't, then what? Or what if she changes her mind and calls the police? Then I gotta split."

"No, don't say that. You can't go."

"I know. We gotta get Sky going."

Finny wanted to tell him that that wasn't what she

meant, that it hadn't even occurred to her. The thought of him out of her life was unbearable. She brushed her hair behind her ear, struggling with how to say it.

"I just need to get a job. Once I do, I'll feel better."

"Let's try next door. Jeff is really busy. He has grooms, but no one to help train his young horses. I have my lesson today anyway. Come with me. It's worth a try."

"Okay."

Finny gave Sky a good-bye pat and she and Joe made their way to Silver Spur. As they walked up the drive, they spotted Carl.

"Look, there he is. I'd like to punch him three hundred dollars worth."

"I don't recommend it," Finny said with a quick laugh. "Besides, I don't think he'd recognize you. In the last six weeks you've gained weight and I swear you got taller."

"Yeah?"

Finny nodded. Joe smiled; he'd take growing a bit. They walked past Carl with no hassles. Joe figured Finny was right.

"I gotta see who I'm riding. I'll be right back."

Joe sat on the large cushioned bench in the spotless barn aisle. Around the corner came Elsa.

"Well, well, look who's back."

"Hi, Elsa."

"So, to what do we owe the honor of your presence?"

"Same as before, looking for work."

"So my 'work' wasn't good enough?"

"I need a real job."

"Joe, I know you do." Elsa sat next to him. "I really was just trying to be nice and give you a hand until you found one. I didn't mean to be . . . pushy." Joe was surprised; she sounded sincere. Maybe he'd misread her.

"As a matter of fact, I'll go talk to Jeff right now."

"You don't have to, Elsa, really."

"Don't be silly—it will ensure that you get hired." Elsa patted Joe's unbraced knee and went to find Jeff. A moment later Finny came around the corner leading an older flea-bitten gray horse.

"Finny, Elsa said she'd hook me up with a job here. She went to go talk with Jeff." A jealous anger instantly lit in Finny; she mentally damped it down.

"Well, it would be the first time she'd ever been useful."

"You really don't like her do you?"

"She's just gone out of her way to make my life miserable for the last four years and I have no idea why."

"She's jealous of you, that's why."

"Jealous of what? She has everything. I have nothing."

"I've never hung out much with other kids, so I can't

a smile and walked away. Finny saw Joe blush. He liked Elsa. Why wouldn't he? She was beautiful and in two minutes she had given Joe everything he wanted. Who wouldn't fall for her? Finny knew she was doing it again. Her emotions were somersaulting in her head like a crazy person. She knew Joe liked her as a friend. Boys liked her like a buddy. Now she knew why—she was really cool without trying.

"Finny, can you believe it? A job and a place to live? It's all working out."

"Yes, it's all perfect." Finny led the horse to the mounting block and got on.

"Is everything okay?"

"Everything's great." Not meeting Joe's eye, Finny kicked her horse forward and trotted to the arena. After a moment of confusion Joe followed to watch.

Ivey, Katie, and Kayla were already in the field warming up their horses. Jeff typically worked thirty minutes on the flat and the girls knew to get their horses limber and ready.

Ivey cantered her horse up to Finny. "Hi, Finny. Is that Nemo?"

"It sure is."

"You're so lucky."

Finny had to laugh; Ivey's horse was beautiful and won at the shows all the time. Nemo was Jeff's former

Grand Prix horse and although he didn't jump high anymore, the kids all thought he was the greatest.

"I hope Jeff lets me ride him sometime," Ivey said with longing.

"Ask him. I bet he'd let you." Ivey's eyes got huge. She shook her head as if that was a crazy idea.

"He's too scary."

Finny laughed again. She understood; Jeff could be intimidating even when he was in a good mood. Katie and Kayla trotted over to Finny and Ivey.

"Who's that?" Kayla was staring over Finny's shoulder. Finny craned her head around. "Oh, that's my friend Joe."

"Is he your boyfriend?" Katie asked. She looked impressed.

"No, just a friend."

"Oh." All three girls looked disappointed.

"He's cute. Cuter than Dale even. How come he's not your boyfriend?" Ivey asked.

"Okay, girls, track left, posting trot." Jeff came into the field barking out the order. The three younger girls instantly separated and put their horses to work. Finny was grateful for Jeff's timing. She nudged Nemo in the sides and put him into a working trot.

"Shoulder in, down the long side," Jeff shouted. Nemo, expertly trained, moved his shoulder away from Finny's outside leg with just a feather touch.

"Excellent, Finny." Compliments from him, which were few and far between, always thrilled her.

She trotted past Joe leaning on the fence watching her ride. She felt like a jerk for getting mad. He was a wonderful friend and if that was all, then that was better than nothing. Maybe someday she'd figure out boys and even get a boyfriend, she told herself. But as much as she tried to make things right in her head, she knew watching Joe slowly fall in love with Elsa would do her in.

"Finny! Finny, look!" It was Joe. He was pointing toward Azure Hills. Finny and everyone in the arena turned to look. Sky was cantering toward the Silver Spur ring. He had jumped out of not only the stallion pen but the fence that separated the two properties. Sky was heading toward the flood control channel. Finny caught her breath, panicked he'd fall in if he tried to jump it. Sky slammed on the brakes at the channel. He looked down and snorted, then did what he always did when aggravated—he pawed at the ground viciously.

In horror, Finny watched him trot in a circle and blast off toward the channel.

"No!" Finny screamed. In her head she saw Sky crashing, his legs breaking. Sky was cantering now, only strides away from the channel. His ears were pricked forward. Finny watched as his muscles bunched. Then Sky launched himself. The distance was at least fifteen feet. He cleared it with ease, landing softly on the other side. The other students gasped. Finny left the field quickly and rode Nemo toward Sky, who cantered up to her with a snort and danced around her. Joe came as fast as he could with a halter and lead.

"Whoa, boy, settle down." Joe did his best to get Sky to stop as he trotted around Nemo.

"Finny, hop down. He'll stop for you."

She dismounted and Sky came up to her. She patted his nose. Joe slipped on the halter.

"Did you see him jump that?" Joe pointed toward the culvert.

"I did. I don't know whether to be happy or horrified."

Jeff came up to Joe and Finny. "Finny, whose horse is this?"

"He's mine. I keep him next door."

"Did you see him jump? If you have a horse that can jump like this why aren't you lessoning on him?"

"He's not broke yet."

Jeff ran his hand down Sky's neck and shoulder. "He looks warmblood."

"He's half warmblood, half thoroughbred."

"This is a nice horse. Why don't you bring him tomorrow and we'll put him through the jump chute? Let's find out what he's capable of."

"You mean it?"

"Yeah, bring him by at eleven."

"Okay, Jeff. Wow, thank you." With a final pat for Sky, Jeff turned and went back to the other girls, who were standing stock still on their horses in the jump field.

"Joe, did you hear that?"

"I don't know if this is a good idea, Finny. It may be too soon."

"Why? Sky obviously loves to jump and Jeff wants to work with him. Do you know what this means?"

"Not really."

"Jeff Hastings has the finest show jumpers in the state. He'd never waste his time if he didn't think a horse had serious potential."

"I understand . . . I just think it's too soon."

"Why?"

"It's just my gut. He doesn't like to listen to people. I'm afraid anything Jeff does will backfire."

"He's been training horses for years. I'm sure he knows what he's doing."

Elsa, who was hacking in the main arena, had watched the whole scene from the back of her stunning, fire red Grand Prix horse, Savannah. She rode over to Joe and Finny. "I can't believe this is the same horse I watched you drag across the road." Elsa gave Sky a once-over. Finny didn't comment. She didn't want to battle in front of Joe.

"I'll take him home," Joe said, giving Sky a pat and leading him toward the road.

"Hold up, Joe. I'll walk with you." Elsa hopped off Savannah and shoved her reins into Finny's hand.

"Put my horse away," Elsa ordered before running to catch up to Joe. Finny's aggravation mounted as she watched them leave. She didn't know what Elsa was up to and didn't know why Joe wasn't supportive of Jeff working with Sky. He knew it was everything she'd wanted. Finny turned both horses back to the barn. Now with Elsa's horse to care for, she couldn't finish her lesson.

Once done untacking and hosing down Nemo, Finny took care of Savannah while periodically checking the fence line for Joe. By the time she was done, it was almost dark and Joe hadn't come back.

Finny headed for Azure Hills. There was enough light to see the board Joe had nailed up over the stallion pen gate. That must have been where Sky had jumped out. Finny called Joe's name a few times and searched for him. He was nowhere to be found. At the house she knocked on Vel's door.

"Hey, Finny. You're here late."

"I'm looking for Joe. Have you seen him?"

"He left in a car a few minutes ago."

"Oh. Did he say where he was going?"

Vel let out a laugh. "Finny, he hardly speaks, so I couldn't tell you."

"Okay, well, thanks, I'll see you tomorrow." Finny began her solitary walk home in the dark. She couldn't believe Joe would just ditch her. She wanted to go to the trailer to see if he was there, to talk to him, to make sure he was okay and not in love with Elsa, but half of her didn't want to. If he could forget her so fast, and be all into Elsa, then they deserved each other.

It was a miserable walk home and late when Finny finally walked through the door. The house was dark and Finny bumped into something in the hall. She clicked on the lights and saw all the suitcases out and ready for the trip. It felt like a knife twisted in her side. She ran up the stairs and collapsed on her bed. Her head began to pound. Finny grabbed her pillow and pressed it over her head, then took several deep breaths and willed herself not to cry. But cry she did, wrenching sobs that actually hurt. She grabbed her midsection and curled up, positive she was dying. Finny tried not to think of Joe with Elsa and what they were doing. She tried not to think of her family that didn't want her sending her to her other family that didn't want her. Weary and worn out, she drifted off into a restless sleep.

Chapter Nine

———————

GETTING OUT OF BED WAS A STRUGGLE. FINny's heartache from the night before left her weary. She dragged herself into the shower and let the warm water pound the tension out of her shoulders. Not wanting to face the day, she stayed in the shower long after the water went cold. When she began to shiver, she shut off the water and wrapped herself in a robe. The mirror reflected back an ashen face. Finny let out a sigh and grabbed her never-opened tube of mascara. It didn't take a genius to figure out how to use it and in no time she was admiring her new look. Finny put some eyeliner on next, realizing it should have gone on first, but tomorrow she'd do it right. A little bit of foundation was next and then some blush. Now with her color back, Finny felt the blush was too much and washed it off. She grabbed the blow-dryer and dried her hair. Normally air and time dried it, letting her hair curl just a bit. With the blow-dryer she could make it dead straight. Once styled, her hair fell around her shoulders like a halo of amber. Finny was tempted to leave it down but she knew it'd be too hot so she made a ponytail high on her head and used a shiny gold tie to secure it.

Happy with her new look, Finny got dressed and headed down the stairs. After grabbing a breakfast bar and some orange juice, Finny left on her bike for Azure Hills. She'd normally go to the trailer but since Joe hadn't waited for her last night, she didn't want to go the extra miles if he wasn't there.

Sky nickered loudly and began to paw the ground with his hoof as soon as he saw Finny. She patted his neck and looked around for Joe. There was no sign of him. Guilt settled in. Finny knew she should have gone to the trailer but he should have waited for her last night. She let out a moan and grabbed a feed bucket. He'd figure it out and come. Then she could tell him she was sorry and find out why he left without her. By now Finny was thinking reasonably and just wanted to get it all cleared up. She settled into her morning routine of chores.

It was close to eleven, time to take Sky next door for his training session with Jeff. Finny began to worry. She'd had second thoughts about taking him since Joe was so against it. Nevertheless, she had groomed Sky until he was immaculate and wrapped his legs with clean polo wraps in preparation. She looked at her watch; it was time to go and no Joe. A bit of anger crept in because he wasn't there. She took one last look for Joe then clipped on Sky's lead line and headed for Silver Spur.

She and Sky arrived just on time. Jeff was waiting for her by the small arena that had a jump chute attached to it.

"Hello, Finny."

"Hi, Jeff. Thank you so much for doing this."

"No problem. I'd like to see what you got here."

Elsa wandered over to watch. Finny wished she could ask her to go away but that would be a big no-no. She looked around for Joe.

"New hair tie, Finny?" Elsa baited. Finny self-consciously touched her gold tie. "Super sale at the thrift store?" Elsa asked with a smirk. Finny ignored her and led Sky over to Jeff.

Jeff took the lead and brought Sky into the ring. Just then Finny spotted Joe coming her way. He didn't have his crutch and his immobilizer was off. He was walking limp free. Her pulse quickened at the sight of him. Elsa noticed, too, hurried over to Joe, and whispered something in his ear. Joe's shoulders sagged a bit, but he nodded and changed course toward the barn. Elsa looked toward Finny, smiled big, and took off after him. Finny slowly counted to ten and turned her attention back to Sky. Jeff was trying to get Sky to move around him in a circle.

"Finny, he can lunge, can't he?"

"Yes, but he likes to do things on his own terms. I sorta talk him into lunging."

"Well, that's going to change." With that Jeff took the lunge whip and cracked it across Sky's hindquarters. Sky froze a moment before blasting off across the arena, ripping the lunge line out of Jeff's hand. Finny ran into the arena and tried to get Sky to stop. Joe dashed from the barn and joined Finny.

Elsa strolled out to watch, a small sliver of a smile on her face. Finally, Joe managed to corner Sky and stop him. Jeff came stomping over to Joe who was quietly reassuring the horse and jerked the line out of his hand.

"This thing needs to learn some manners."

"Jeff, he's twelve and doesn't think like a horse." Joe's words of warning fell on deaf ears. Jeff put Sky in the jumping chute, then lashed him across his hindquarters again. Instead of going forward Sky staggered backward and fell to the ground. Finny ran to him crying.

"Kids, you've spoiled this thing rotten. He's not hurt, he's throwing a tantrum."

"Finny," Joe whispered frantically, "let's get him out of here." Finny nodded and grabbed the line, begging Sky to get up. Jeff came over, whip in hand. The horse took one look, leapt to his feet, and charged Jeff, smashing him to the ground.

"Oh God!" Finny gasped and ran to Jeff. "Elsa, call nine-one-one." Elsa grabbed her phone and dialed, then rushed to Jeff's side. Sky continued to tear around the ring at breakneck speed, the lunge line trailing out behind him. Sky slid to a stop, spun the other way, and opened up his stride. Finny knew he was going to jump out and he did. But the lunge line snagged between two boards and when Sky hit the end of the line, he flipped, rolling one time before landing in a heap outside the arena. He didn't move. Finny left Jeff, who lay moaning, with Elsa and took off after her horse. Joe was right behind her.

"Is he dead, Joe? Tell me, I can't look." Finny knelt by her horse with her hands over her eyes. Joe put his cheek to Sky's muzzle and felt a faint breath.

"He's alive."

"Oh God, Joe, why isn't he moving? Stay with him, I gotta check on Jeff." Finny ran back to Jeff, who was sitting up but clearly in pain.

"Finny that maniac horse of yours almost killed him." Elsa's voice was high and tight as she yelled, "This is all your fault." Finny apologized profusely to Jeff. He waved her off with his right hand, but didn't speak. She jumped up and ran back to Sky and Joe. She heard sirens in the distance, and within minutes an ambulance was speeding across the lawn followed by a fire truck.

"Joe, you told me not to come. Oh God, what am I going to do?" Finny sobbed and gently ran her fingers down Sky's face.

"Finny, it's going to be okay. I think he's just knocked out. And Jeff's okay. Look, he's sitting up talking to the paramedics." Joe didn't think Finny even heard him, she was so distraught.

"Sky, come on, buddy. I know you're alive." Joe kept patting Sky's neck. The horse's eyes moved; a moment later he lifted his head.

Joe stepped back. Sky, beginning to rouse slowly, staggered to his feet.

"He's up."

Finny nodded in a daze; she looked over to Jeff. The paramedics were loading him into the ambulance. Then the doors closed and the ambulance sped off.

"Get that thing out of here," Elsa shrieked, "before he hurts anyone else."

"Can he walk?" Finny asked Joe.

"We can try. But, do you see how his eye rolls every few seconds?"

"Yes."

"That's a sign of a brain injury, like a concussion."

"Is he going to be okay?"

"I don't know. I've only seen this one other time."

"What happened to that horse?"

"That other horse was a lot worse off than Sky. He was bleeding from his ears and nose and he hit his head much harder."

"The horse died, didn't it?"

"Yeah, but Sky looks better already. Let's see if we can get him home." After a gentle tug Sky moved forward but lurched from side to side as if dizzy.

"Why didn't I listen to you Joe? You said not to bring him here."

"It's not your fault. If I had been here sooner I could have explained to Jeff Sky's thinking process. Then he wouldn't have used the whip—at least I think he wouldn't have."

"Where were you?"

"I was at the trailer. I waited for you, but you never came. So I went to Azure Hills and finally Silver Spur. Why didn't you come to the trailer?"

"Joe, I'm sorry. You didn't come back last night. I didn't know if you'd be there or maybe Elsa found you someplace else. I don't know what I was thinking."

"I did come back. Elsa took me on another stupid

wild-goose chase. I swear I'll never get in a car again with that girl. When she finally brought me back to Azure Hills you'd already left. I walked to the trailer. I'm sorry, she said she needed my help for just a minute . . . didn't know it'd be over an hour."

Sky was walking better, his stride smoothing out.

Finny sighed. "I should have known better. Anything Elsa gets me crazy."

With a shake of his head Joe said, "I don't know about that girl. She says one thing then does another."

Finny let out a small laugh, "It must be exhausting trying to keep it all straight." Joe couldn't help but laugh too.

As they approached Sky's stall, Finny said, "Is he going to be okay? I don't think I have enough money to call the vet."

"I think so. As soon as I get paid, I'll start paying you back. Then I can help you with Sky money-wise, too."

Sky entered his stall and went straight for his pile of hay and began to eat.

"He's gonna be fine," Joe said with relief. "If he didn't feel okay he wouldn't want food."

"Thank God. Thank you, Joe. Thanks for everything you've done. You don't owe me anything."

"You kidding me? Without you I'd still be behind that bus stop."

Finny laughed and shook her head. Joe was doing what he could to make her feel better and it was working.

"I think we should give him a break for a few days, let him totally heal and wait for my leg to be completely ready. Then we'll start again."

"That sounds perfect. Besides, I go to my dad's this weekend."

"You're not going to be here?"

"No. I leave tomorrow night and come back Sunday night. Then school starts. Can you take care of Sky for me while I'm gone?"

"Oh . . . sure. I'll do your chores and all."

"Thanks, Joe. I wish I didn't have to go."

"You don't like going to your dads?"

"Not really. I mean, he's okay . . . it's just . . . different than it used to be."

"I'm sorry."

"No, I'm sorry, at least my parents are here to complain about."

Joe nodded and glanced away. Finny thought he'd stay quiet but this time he didn't.

"They were really in love, my dad and mom. Their parents didn't want them to get married. I think because my mom was Indian and my dad was white."

"Oh, wow. Did their families try to stop them?"

"I think so. I'm not sure what happened but I don't remember ever meeting my dad's parents and before I went to live with my uncle, I'd only ever seen him one other time."

"You're kidding."

Joe eased himself down and sat on the ground. Finny sat down beside him.

"The day after my parents died, he was there. The very first time I saw him, he was fighting my father. I think I was nine. Him and my dad were in an all-out brawl. My mom was screamin' and tryin' to break 'em apart. I didn't think they'd ever stop. My mom finally grabs a shovel and nails my uncle across the head. He goes down and the fight's over."

"How horrible! What was the fight about?"

"No idea. My dad gets up, all bloody. He stands over my uncle and tells him never to set foot on Horse Mountain again."

"Then two years later he shows up and he's your guardian?" Finny asked, eyes wide with shock.

"Yep."

"You must have been terrified."

"I wasn't happy, that's for sure." Joe picked up a rock and rolled it around in his hand.

"What made you finally run?"

"It was time."

Finny knew there had to be more but she'd wait until he was ready to tell her.

"Well I'm glad you did. I think it was meant to be, you coming here."

"I hope so. When I jumped on that trailer, I never thought I'd end up in California."

"Where were you when you got on?"

"Not sure, to tell you the truth. Oklahoma, I think."

"Oh, geez, that's far."

"My uncle followed the rodeo circuit so we traveled all over."

"What did you do for the rodeo?"

"It's where we sold horses. Right before winter we'd round up mustangs and drive them to lower ground. When the spring grasses came they'd graze for thirty days and get fat. I'd break and gentle as many as I could, then come May, we'd take them to the sale. My uncle would cull out what he thought would be good broncs and sell those to the rodeos; the others we'd sell as saddle horses."

"That doesn't sound all bad."

"It wasn't. I mean, I stopped going to school, slept in the backseat of a truck most of the year, which wasn't so great. During the winter I lived on the mountain with the horses. I'd look out for the herd until my uncle sent wranglers up to help bring them in. My uncle stayed in town, wheeling, dealing, drinking, and gambling."

"Actually, Joe, that sounds kinda lonely."

"I got used to it. I'd spend all day every day with the horses. I really got to know 'em and understand how they think and why they behave like they do. They were wild but I could walk with them and touch them. I was accepted as one of their own." Finny grasped Joe's hand and held it in both of hers. She fought back tears even though as Joe told his tale he didn't seem sad. She was struck by how isolated he must have felt with no family, no friends, even in the wonderful world of horses. Finny didn't know what to say, or how Joe felt about her holding his hand. In typical fashion, he didn't show acceptance or rejection. Joe, always the observer, watched and waited. Finny gently squeezed his hand before letting it go.

"I didn't mean to make you cry," Joe said softly.

"I'm sorry. I cry so easily these days."

"Don't worry, once you hit sixteen, all will be better. I'm livin' proof."

Finny dried her eyes with her sleeve and laughed.

"Good."

"It's a milestone, you know, a rite-of-passage age."

Finny laughed again. She wanted to kiss him so badly. He was so handsome and sweet, but she couldn't bring herself to do it—once that line was crossed there'd be no going back.

"Shall we go hit up Vel for lunch?"

"Yep." Joe grabbed his midsection. "I'm starving."

"When aren't you?"

"Good question—never."

Vel hung up the phone. "A separated shoulder, and some torn ligaments."

Finny dropped the rest of her sandwich on her plate and slumped back in the seat.

"It could have been worse; it could have been broken," Vel said, trying to ease Finny's mind. Finny nodded but looked green.

"Kids, I got to run back to work. Lock up when you're done."

"We will, Vel. Thank you for lunch," Joe said.

"Anytime, guys. See you later." Vel dashed off. Joe sat across from Finny.

"Jeff getting hurt will be all Elsa needs to get me kicked out of there."

"Are you serious?"

Finny shrugged. "I don't know. I think Jeff likes me, well *did* anyway."

"I'm sure he still does."

Finny let out a sigh and looked at her watch. "I better head for home."

"So early?"

"I go to my dad's tonight. He wanted me to be ready to go by three."

"Oh. I'll walk you to your house then."

"Are you sure? It's more miles on your leg."

"Yeah, I'm sure. Leg feels great and I'd like to see where you live."

"Okay."

After cleaning up from lunch, Finny and Joe locked the door behind them and headed for Finny's house.

They walked in silence for the first two miles. It was a comfortable silence. They were at ease in each other's company. Mile three, Finny let out a moan.

"What's wrong?"

"I won't see you or Sky till Monday."

Joe nodded his head but said nothing. These were the times that Finny wished he'd say, *Yeah, that's a drag* or *I'll miss you*, but he never did. Finny knew they were friends. She reasoned that just because he didn't say it, didn't mean he didn't feel it.

"So, will you miss me?" Finny couldn't believe she spoke those words out loud. She closed her eyes and got ready for the laugh or the startled answer.

"Sure will," he stated simply, like it went without saying. She immediately felt better, lighter, happy.

Finny groaned internally. She realized fully the profound effect Joe's presence had on her. She had become her most feared stereotype: a certified lunatic, completely hung up on a boy and apparently hopeless. Two days without him—she didn't think she could take it.

They stopped in front of a quaint blue and white-trimmed two-story house. The perfectly maintained lawn stretched up a short hill to a small white porch.

"This is where I live."

"Oh, wow, it's so big and beautiful."

"This is a typical tract home. If you want big you should see Elsa's."

Joe continued to study the house and the surrounding neighborhood, mapping it out in his head.

"You want to go inside?"

"What about your mom?"

"She's not home, but even if she was, it'd be cool."

They walked up the drive, through the garage, past a mountain of toddler toys the twins no longer played with, and into the kitchen.

"Want some cookies or something? There's a lot of little-kid-friendly food here."

"Sure, anything."

Finny searched around the cupboard and pulled out some cookies, then milk from the fridge. She placed it in front of Joe who was still wide-eyed, surveying the room.

She sat down at the kitchen table to eat with him.

"I hope you don't mind, but I asked my mom for any clothes my stepdad didn't want. I told her it was for a friend. They're in a bag by the closet."

"Clothes? Do you think they'll fit?"

"Close enough." Finny saw he was excited. She got up and grabbed the bag.

"These are so great. If my T-shirts get any more holes they'll be more holes than shirt." Joe was searching the bag thoroughly. "Finny, I can start my job not looking like a bum. Thanks again—for the millionth time."

Finny smiled as Joe held up different shirts deciding which one to wear. She propped her elbows on the table, put her chin in her hands, and watched him, disgusted at herself for being so happy.

Chapter Ten

———

JOE LAY IN HIS BED AND LOOKED THROUGH THE window at the stars. He was listening to his birthday gift from Finny. When she handed him the wrapped present yesterday he had to hold back a moan. She had already given him so much it was embarrassing. He opened the box and pulled out the small metal object. He hadn't a clue what it was. "It's an iPod," Finny said. "For listening to music. I put a bunch of songs on it I thought you'd like." Joe looked at the slim object and didn't see how that was possible with no knobs or dials. He knew he had big gaps in knowledge. It wasn't easy keeping up with things when you don't go to school, watch TV, or hang out with other kids your age. He did his best not to let his ignorance show. Joe thanked Finny and slipped it into his pocket. Finny, with one eyebrow raised, put her hand out, palm up. Joe took it out of his pocket and put it in her hand. She showed him how it worked. At first he was startled at the amazing sound. Within two minutes he was mesmerized.

Joe turned off the iPod and put it away. He arranged his pillows so he could see outside the window more easily. The stars were different this far west. He knew the constellations his father had taught him. Joe went through the ones he could see. He didn't want to forget anything his parents had told him. He wondered where, in the mass of stars, heaven was. Joe said a silent prayer to his parents, thanking them for leading him to California, for leading him to Finny.

He had a plan. He'd start his job, begin to make money and support himself. He wanted to train Sky to perfection. Then he wanted to buy Finny nice things and take her out on a date in a car and treat her right. Once he could do those things he'd ask her to be his girlfriend. The thought sent a chill down his spine. He closed his eyes tight, to shut out the worry that she was only around because he was pitiful and needed help as much as her horse. Joe didn't want to be her project. He knew she felt bad for him. He didn't want her to feel bad, to feel pity. Could you love someone you pitied? Joe didn't think so.

As soon as Finny arrived at her dad's house, her half brother and sister dashed from their rooms and jumped on her.

"Finny, come see my new goldfish!" Four-year-old Jordan was trying to drag her to his room.

"Okay, okay, I'm coming!" She picked up her two-year-old sister who had clamped onto her leg.

"They love when you come," Linda, Finny's step-mother, told her. Finny thought Linda, petite and pretty, with brown hair and eyes, bore a striking resemblance to her mother.

"Let's go, guys. I can't wait to see your fish." Her brother led the way. Finny kept her hyper siblings entertained and by dinnertime they had finally settled so they all could sit down to eat.

"Hey Daddy, I showed Finny my fish! She liked it."

"That's 'cause she has good taste, Jordan." Finny's dad gave her a wink then said, "So, we have a birthday coming up."

Finny nodded and hoped the conversation would lead in the direction of a cell phone. A new saddle would have been nice, too, but she knew her dad wouldn't be any more receptive to that idea than her mom would be.

"Have you thought of what you'd like?" Her dad was nonchalant when he asked. Every year since she had the ability to speak she'd asked for a horse. Didn't need that now.

"I know it's a lot but is there a chance of getting a cell phone?"

"Cell phone? I was expecting you to ask for a horse," Linda said.

"I've asked for a horse for the last ten years. It's time to move on." Finny felt her face flush. She studied her food. She hated to lie. Or at least not tell the full truth.

"That's very mature of you, Finny," her dad said.

"So, does that mean I'm mature enough for a phone? I'm, like, the only kid on the planet without one. I'd keep the bill down, I promise," Finny reasoned.

"I'll think about it. Pass the ketchup, please."

Finny did, and then let the conversation drop. *I'll think about it* usually meant *no*.

By the time dinner was over the kids were anxious to play so they dashed off and her dad went to spend time with them. This gave Finny some alone time with Linda. She wanted to ask her an important question, even though she was feeling guilty about it. If her mom knew she'd gone to Linda, instead of her, she would be very hurt.

"Hey, Linda, can I talk to you about something?"

"Sure, Finny. Can you bring the dinner plates from the table?"

Finny picked up as many plates as she could carry and put them on the counter. Linda was putting away the leftovers in the fridge.

"Give them a good rinse before putting them in the dishwasher."

"Okay . . . So Linda, how do you know, or like how can you tell, if you're in love?" Linda closed the refrigerator door and looked at Finny with a bemused smile.

"Finny, you're too young to be in love."

Finny chewed her lip and let out a quiet but frustrated breath. She was hoping for more than a pat answer. Finny rinsed the dinner plates and set them in the dishwasher. She thought again about asking her mom. She just didn't want to deal with the questions. Who is he, how did you meet, where does he live? What makes you think you're in love? Or even worse questions that were sure to follow. How serious are you, have you kissed him, do we need to have *the talk*?

Finny looked up to try one more time with Linda, but she had left the room.

Chapter Eleven

———

THE SUN WAS SETTING, ENDING NOT ONLY THE day but the summer. It was Sunday night and Finny had her father drop her off at Azure Hills instead of home. She wanted to see Sky and Joe. School was starting tomorrow and Finny couldn't have been less excited. The summer of her fourteenth year would be hard to forget, her dream come true. She had a horse of her own and on top of that a best friend. Finny spotted Joe leaning into Sky's corral, watching him.

"Hey, Joe."

Startled by her voice, he turned quickly and a smile lit up his face. Finny's heart flipped in her chest. *He must like me as more than a friend*, she thought.

"Hey, Finny! Sky's doing great. He seems settled down. You know, I think that fall seemed to have knocked some sense into him."

"It would be nice if something good came from that day."

"Hey, wanna check out my new trailer?"

Finny gave Sky a pat and a carrot and the two made their way to Silver Spur. They chose to walk the road instead of the field.

"Look how the broken glass pieces along the road shine like diamonds." Joe dislodged some and sent them flying with a quick stab from his toe.

"I wish they were diamonds. That'd solve every-thing," Finny said.

"What's to solve? Everything's perfect. I have a home and a job, and Sky is going to be okay." Finny realized Joe was right. On top of that, he was happy. When he smiled big, dimples appeared.

"You're right, Joe, totally right. I'm going to miss hanging out all day with you though."

"Me too, Finny, but I got to work, and you got school."

"How's your leg feel? It's four days now without the immobilizer, right?"

"Feels perfect." Joe dashed off a few steps, spun, and ran back. Finny laughed at his display.

"Don't go overboard."

"You kiddin' me? I am a model of self-control. I wanted to run all the way, but see, walkin'.'"

"I'm amazed by your restraint." Joe's good mood was rubbing off. She was glad he was happy. Joe deserved to be happy. They made it through the gates and down the driveway. The mobile home that was now Joe's stood well behind the main barn, near Carl and Ray's small house.

"Have you been in it yet?"

"Yep, I checked it out. I figure with your trailer now for sale, I'd better stop taking my chances there and get moved in here."

"You're right. We've been lucky."

"Wanna race the rest of the way?"

"Joe, don't be silly. You need to save your leg," Finny said, then blasted off full speed toward the trailer.

"Oh, not fair!" Joe took off too. Once at the door Finny let Joe pass to go in first. He turned the knob; with a loud squeak of protesting hinges, the door opened. The first thing they encountered was the smell: mildew and stale air.

"We need to open all the windows," Finny gasped.

The trailer had three rooms and six windows total. Once they were opened, breathing was possible. There was no furniture, just dirt and trash.

"Finny, can you believe this?"

"No."

"Isn't it incredible?"

"Oh, uh, yes. It's great." Finny realized she and Joe had wildly different definitions of *incredible*. Joe wandered through all the rooms, then opened the cabinets in the kitchen.

"I know it needs cleanin', but this is my home." Joe crossed his arms and surveyed the place. His smile said it all.

"First thing as soon as I'm back from school, let's clean it top to bottom. Then we got to get you some furniture."

"I get paid in two weeks, Finny. Two weeks and I'll be set."

Chapter Twelve

———————

AT 6 AM THE ALARM RANG. FINNY GOT OUT of bed and was showered and dressed before 6:30. She got up earlier than normal. Doing hair and makeup took a little more time. Finny liked how she looked with makeup. If anything, she looked older. In one week she would be; she'd turn fifteen. Finny put her lip gloss in her pocket because it wouldn't survive breakfast and went downstairs. The kitchen was empty. Finny's heart tugged in her chest. She chewed on her lip and listened for her mother. All quiet. Throughout the summer she had made her own breakfast and done her own thing. But on her first day of school Finny thought her mom would at least be down to say, "Have a good day!" or something.

Finny poured some cereal and milk and sat at the table. She heard the chatter of her sisters and some thumps coming from their room above. She knew her mom would be up attending to them soon. After putting her dishes in the sink, Finny grabbed her backpack and went upstairs. She found her mom in her sisters' room.

"Hey, Mom, I'm heading off to school."

Beth gave up trying to get one of the twins to come out from under the bed and stood to hug Finny. "Have a wonderful day, honey." She held Finny at arm's reach. "You look so beautiful, and how you do your eye make-up is really elegant."

"Thanks, Mom."

"Do you have everything you need?"

Finny patted her backpack. "I do."

"Okay, baby. Have fun."

Finny, feeling better, went to the bus stop and waited. A few kids she recognized from the neighborhood made their way to the stop. She hadn't given them a thought all summer. Her world was the stables now. She said hello, but like her, no one seemed too excited to be there.

Day one of school turned out to be uneventful. Finny got her new locker and all her books and managed to get to her classes on time. She typically got good grades and liked school, but today was a countdown. Every minute that ticked by put her closer to Joe and Sky.

When the bell rang, Finny grabbed her books, bolted from the classroom, and crashed right into someone. It was Dale, from the feed store.

"Sorry, I didn't see you." Finny was terribly embarrassed; she'd all but knocked him down.

"Don't be. I should know when the bell rings to watch out." Finny laughed, then hugged her books to her chest.

"Well, sorry again. I'll see you later."

"No problem, Finny. I'll see you tomorrow." He waved, smiled, and left. Finny shoved her books in her pack and swung it over her shoulder. Dale knew her name? That was a surprise. She went to the buses and found the one that would leave her close to Azure Hills. Once it dropped her off, Finny dashed around doing her chores as quickly as she could so she could get to Silver Spur.

Finny rinsed out the last feed bucket and put it away. She wiped her brow and hoped she didn't look like a mess. Elsa always looked perfect no matter what. But then, Elsa never lifted a finger or broke a sweat. She grabbed her backpack that was weighed down with cleaning supplies for Joe's trailer and went to find him. And find him she did. He was leaning up against the wall in the barn, Elsa standing in front of him, a little too close for Finny's liking. They were talking quietly.

Finny walked up and heard Elsa say, "This is a nice look on you." Then to her horror Elsa ran her hand across his shoulder and down the middle of his chest as if straightening his shirt. Finny walked up and when Joe saw her, his eyes got big. She didn't know if it was from guilt, embarrassment, happiness, or what. All she knew was she was mad—at him, Elsa, herself, and the world in general. Joe slid sideways a step to remove himself from Elsa, but not before she grabbed his hand and held it in both of hers. "Joe, I had an amazing afternoon. Thank you, you are doing wonders for our horses."

"No problem." Joe stood until Elsa, who was holding his hand for an excessively long time, released it. Elsa didn't bother to even smirk at Finny. She just turned and walked away.

Joe gave Finny a crooked smile, knowing she'd be mad.

"So what was that all about?" Finny crossed her arms and stared at Joe. Seeing his face, remembering that all things Elsa made her crazy, she put her hands up to stop him from whatever he was going to say. "I'm sorry . . . I'm going to start again. Hi, Joe, how are you?"

Joe smiled again. "I can't complain. How are you?"

"Glad to be here!"

"How was school?"

"Boring."

"That's too bad. You ready to go to Sky?"

"Sure, but I have cleaning supplies for the trailer."

"About that . . . I gotta show you something."

Joe led Finny to the trailer and opened the door, which swung smoothly from its fixed hinges. The trailer was spotless top to bottom and nicely furnished.

"How did this happen?"

"Don't be mad.

"Elsa," Finny said, monotone.

Joe nodded his head. "When I came, Jeff was waiting for me. He showed me the trailer, told me it was compliments of the Davenports. Then, he told me all the young horses he has are in partnership with Elsa's dad. So he wants me to work with her and teach her how to handle them properly."

"Oh . . . so that's what she was talking about, her amazing afternoon?"

Joe laughed and shook his head. "Yeah, not sure what made it amazing though."

Finny did. It was being with Joe that made any day amazing. Maybe Elsa truly liked him and wasn't just flirting with him to irritate her. Finny couldn't believe she wouldn't go for some rich boy with a fancy car. But no rich boy she knew was as sweet as Joe. Plus, his complete lack of ego was refreshing. No "I'm hot and I know it" attitude.

"Hey, Joe . . ." Finny wanted to ask, "So, do you like her? Will you fall for her? What about me? I'm crazy about you, but I can't say it for some reason. I know we're friends, but will we ever be more, do you want it to be more?" Instead she finished with, "Are you ready to go see Sky?"

"Yep! Today's he's going to be great, Finny. I can feel it."

"Remember, if he starts to buck and play just slide off."

Finny was ready to mount Sky for the first time. He'd had two weeks under saddle and bridle and had learned to accept them.

Joe led Sky to the mounting block.

"Just lay over him on your belly," Joe instructed. Finny climbed the block. She gave Sky a pat.

"Okay, here goes." Finny gently lay over Sky's back.

"Perfect. Now rub his belly and talk to him."

"Good boy, Sky. You're a good horse." Finny patted him and was proud he was standing quietly.

"Okay, Finny, hang on. I'm going to lead him now." Finny held onto the saddle. She felt funny riding her horse on her belly but he was moving, carrying her weight and not bucking her off. She wasn't taking a good thing for granted and patted him the entire time. At this rate, she reasoned, she'd be astride him in a week.

"Finny, that's perfect. Hop off. I think he's done enough for today." Finny slid to the ground almost falling, forgetting how big Sky was.

"Joe, I rode him! Can you believe it? I was on my horse!" Finny jumped up and down and grabbed Joe in a hug. Joe didn't hug back but he didn't tense up either. Finny broke the hug and hoped he didn't mind that she hugged him. Besides, Elsa put her hands all over him every chance she got. It didn't look like that bugged him. *Ugh*, truth be told, *she couldn't tell what he made of Elsa's attentions.*

"The next few days'll tell us a lot. The first couple of tries a horse is usually good because he doesn't know what's going on," Joe said.

"I hope he stays good."

Finny and Joe untacked Sky and put him in his stall. They worked well together, each knowing intuitively what the other needed.

"Finny, next week I want to get on the colts next door. Will you help me? I'd like you there to handle them while I mount."

"Sure, Joe, I'd love to. What about Elsa, won't she want to?"

"I don't know, but I need you. I got to have someone who knows what they're doing." Joe stated it simply, unaware that it made Finny's heart soar.

Chapter Thirteen

THE TEACHER DRONED ON ABOUT MOLECULAR structure. Finny was trying to pay attention. She was trying to enjoy school. She used to enjoy school. Finny tried again to focus. Finally, after what seemed like a lifetime had passed, the bell rang, ending the school day. Finny rushed to her locker. Dale was there opening the one next to hers.

"Oh, hey there, Finny. I hear you have a horse now."

"Uh, yes. I do." First he knew her name, and now about Sky? Finny was officially stunned. How could he possibly know?

"That's great. So, you keep him at Silver Spur?"

"No, I just take lessons there. I never could afford to board there. My horse is next door at Azure Hills."

"I'm delivering feed there in a couple of days. I'd love to see him."

Finny bit her lip. This was too weird. "Sure, anytime."

"Great! I'll see you later." Finny watched him go, wondering why she was suddenly no longer invisible.

Finny hurried to the bus. Forty-five minutes later she was at Azure Hills. Joe was waiting for her and had Sky tacked up and ready.

"Wow, talk about service," Finny said.

"No problem. Working next door is a breeze. I get done pretty fast, then come over here and work."

"Once we're done with Sky I can finish up anything you didn't have time to do."

"No need, did it all."

"You're kidding me."

"Nope, I work fast."

"I see that—you're going to get me fired!"

"Oh, Finny, I'm sorry! I'd never do that."

"Joe, I'm kidding."

Joe's relief was visible. He took off the halter that was over Sky's bridle and led him into the arena. Finny grabbed her helmet and put it on. Joe lined up Sky to the mounting block and after a few pats and rubs Finny lay over his back.

"Ready?" Joe said, holding Sky's bridle.

"Yes." Joe began to lead Sky. The horse walked along, not at all bothered by Finny's one hundred and eighteen pounds.

"You okay to go around the ring once like that, Finny?"

"Yes, doing fine. Good boy, Sky, for not bucking Mommy off." Finny patted his side.

"Okay," Joe said when they'd gone once around. "Go for it. Swing your leg and sit on him." Finny did and Sky didn't flinch. Joe continued to lead Sky around the arena.

"Joe, this is a miracle! Can you believe it? A miracle. I'm riding Sky." Finny closed her eyes and felt the horse beneath her. His stride even at the walk was long and smooth. He was comfortable to sit on and he felt like he fit her leg just right. She glanced around from her high perch and noticed how wonderful everything looked. Finny stroked Sky's long neck and told him he was the most beautiful horse she'd ever seen.

"Okay, hop down." Finny did as softly as she could and then gave Sky a hug. Joe thought Finny glowed with joy and that made his day.

Chapter Fourteen

GLITTERY POSTERS ADORNED THE WALLS. THE Fall Formal was coming up: A dance, Finny thought, at the high school where all the pretty cheerleaders dressed up and danced with all the pretty football players so they could lord their greatness over the common folk, also known as the average student. It was cliché central and Finny found herself at odds. Last year even under the threat of torture and death she would never have gone. Now she sort of wanted to go. Done for the day, Finny put her books in her locker. She looked at the poster again. She reasoned her mom would finally stop hounding her if she proved she wasn't a complete social outcast and went to a dance with a boy.

She pictured herself showing up with super-handsome Joe on her arm. All dressed up in a suit and tie with his hair slicked back. She'd ask her mom to take her shopping to buy a beautiful dress. Her fantasy screeched to a halt. She didn't know how to dance, and would be stunned if Joe did . . . or if he'd even go, or if a non-student *could* go. Finny looked once more at the sign and sighed. A tap on her shoulder took her attention.

"Hey, Finny."

"Oh, hi Dale."

"I wanted to tell you I go right by your ranch on the way to work so I can give you a ride if you want. Save you from the bus."

"Really? That'd be great! Thanks." Finny followed him to his BMW convertible. Like Elsa, Dale was one of the social elite. He had his feed store job for two reasons. One, his dad owned the store and most of the town. And two, his father wasn't going to raise a lazy, spoiled kid so he put Dale to work.

Finny worked at appearing nonchalant when she got in the car. She wanted to "ooh" and "ahh" all over its soft leather seats, but didn't want to look like a dork.

"Your car's sweet."

"Thanks, Finny. Would you like the top up or down?"

Nice of him to give her a choice, she thought. "Down would be great." She'd never ridden in a convertible and was excited. Fifteen minutes later they were pulling into Silver Spur. Finny checked her watch. This put her

"Yeah, sure, I'm fine."

"Okay. You just seem, I don't know, sorta sad." Joe looked over his shoulder at Finny. He gave her a smile that didn't reach his eyes, telling her she was right when he tried to convince her she was wrong.

"You'd tell me if something was wrong, wouldn't you?"

"Sure I would." Joe gave Sky a pat on the neck but didn't look back at her. *I'll give him some time*, Finny thought. *Let him work out whatever it is, then I'll ask again.*

"What about taking him off the line? See if I can walk him around a little without being led."

"Go for it. It's time." Joe unhooked the lead but stayed by Sky's side as they walked along the fence line.

"See if he will walk in a circle around me. I'll help if he stalls." Finny opened her left rein and closed her right leg, asking Sky to move off it and follow the guiding rein. Sky did so beautifully.

"Now ask him to halt and walk, three times." Sky was slow to react but did as instructed.

"Joe, do you see that? He's listening."

"Yes, I see it. You're doing a great job, Finny."

"Joe, can you believe how good he is?"

"Yeah, but keep in mind, he's hasn't been put under any pressure. When we start to ask for things, that's when he's gonna resist."

"I understand. But Joe, do you think horses can love their owners and treat them better because they do? Does Sky know how much I love him?"

Joe let out a contemplative breath. "That's hard to say. I know horses have emotions and can like and dislike people and things. I just think their instincts trump all. Like, if you were ridin' and your spur accidentally gouged him. He'd react by maybe buckin' you off because he'd react to the pain and try to stop it. He wouldn't think, *Oh I can't buck off my rider 'cause I could hurt her*. I don't think they put the two together. Knowing that will keep you safer. Everyone I know who claimed to have a special way with horses always ended up in the hospital way more than those who didn't."

"Oh wow."

"I do know one thing. If a horse trusts you, you can get a lot more out of him."

"Joe, you are the horse whisperer!"

Joe laughed, "My mom read that book. I remember it from when I was a kid."

"Did your mom like it?"

"Said it was a good story, but found the horse part not so true to life."

Finny slid off Sky and walked him back toward the barn. Halfway there, Vel ran out of her house and up to the kids.

"Joe, Finny, I just got a call for a boarder."

"That's great!" Finny said.

"Gets better—they are looking for someone to work with their horse, help train her up and get her going. I told the man we have the best trainer in the state that just happens to specialize in green horses. Joe, he's coming today to meet you and I hope you don't mind but I told him you charged six hundred a month. That was no problem for him." Joe's mouth hung open in shock.

"Six hundred dollars! Joe, this could be the first of many horses to train once the word gets out," Finny said.

"Really? Six hundred dollars to ride an already broke horse? Unbelievable!" Joe said, still stunned at the news.

"That's per month. He may want several months," Vel said with a big smile.

"Oh man, I gotta get cleaned up! What should I say to him? What if I don't know what to say?"

"I'll meet him with you. We can do it together."

"Thank you, Vel! I'm going to run next door and shower and change. I'll be back in twenty minutes."

"No hurry, you got an hour."

"Thanks again, thanks for everything!" Joe ran to the property line and snaked through the fence; in an instant he was gone.

"Vel, this is so incredible. This could be Joe's big break," Finny said.

"There's a good chance of that. After the man with the horse leaves, I want to sit down with Joe. We need to get a copy of his birth certificate so he can open a bank account. Then he needs to get a driver's license and a social security card. I'm going to offer to help him with everything if he does one thing for me."

"Vel, I'm sure he'll do anything."

"I want him to go back to school."

Chapter Fifteen

———

BETH WAS SITTING ON THE KITCHEN TABLE WHEN Finny walked in the door; she held the school dance flyer in front of her face and shook it.

"I know, Mom. I'm not sure about going."

"Finny, you are going." Beth grabbed her purse. "Steven's watching the girls; you and I are dress shopping!"

"But Mom . . ."

"No buts. Let's go." Beth was so excited it got Finny excited too. She still didn't know what to do about the dance, but her mom wanting to spend time with her, just the two of them, was something Finny didn't want to pass up.

Beth spared no expense. She took Finny to the finest shops the town had to offer. They tried on several dresses. Beth wanted just the right look. Beauty and sophistication without dressing past age-appropriateness. During their outing Finny confessed to her mom that she didn't know how to dance. After one quick phone call, Beth set up a dance lesson for that evening. Finny tried on the next gown. She spun around on the pedestal and loved the silky feel and the look of the dress. Midnight blue, it had a corset-style satin bodice accented with tulle and delicate beadwork. Soft beading trickled down the flowing satiny skirt that fell just below Finny's knees. This dress was the one. She felt like a princess for the first time in her life.

"Finny, you are stunning, baby. Just stunning."

Finny jumped down and hugged her mother. "Thanks, Mom. This is amazing."

"My pleasure, sweetheart. And I want you to know this doesn't count as your birthday present."

"Oh, wow, I'm getting even more stuff?"

Beth let out a laugh at Finny's delight.

"Day after tomorrow you'll know."

Finny was walking on air when she entered the dance studio. Beth had signed her up for five lessons before the dance. After the first it was obvious that Finny, a gifted athlete, had no problems figuring out the moves, her rhythm and timing perfect. By the end of the first lesson she was already confident. That gave her the confidence to finally ask Joe.

She couldn't wait. She headed off to school running over in her head how she was going to ask him. By the time school was out, she'd gone through every possible outcome and answer and still hadn't decided which way to ask. On the way to the buses she spotted Dale waving her over. She bit her lip. She had been avoiding him since the invite.

"I'll give you a ride."

"No, you don't have to."

"Finny, don't be silly. I drive right by, come on."

"Thanks, it saves like an hour. I wish I were turning sixteen instead of fifteen tomorrow so I could get a car."

"Oh, wow, happy sweet fifteen!"

Finny laughed. "Thanks. I'm hoping there will be a sweet cell phone at least. I swear I'm the only kid I know that doesn't have one."

"I don't know how you live without a phone or a car."

"A lot of walking."

"Well, it's kept you in shape, that's for sure." Finny, embarrassed by the compliment, said nothing and willed herself not to turn bright red.

"Since I'm taking you to the ranch, I'd love to see your horse."

"Okay, sure. Do you ride?"

"I rode a pony once when I was a kid but that was it."

"Oh."

"I'd love to learn. Do you think you could teach me?"

"Why, yeah . . . I could do that." Finny was surprised he'd asked, and happy. She wanted to teach people to ride. Dale could be her first student. Finny Miller, riding instructor. She liked the sound of that. If she could teach Dale without killing him that'd prove she could do it.

They pulled into Azure Hills and parked. Finny brought Dale over to the barn. Joe was on a chair waiting. She saw him lock his gaze on Dale.

"Joe, this is Dale from the feed store and school. Dale, this is Joe. He works here and next door and is the greatest trainer you'll ever meet."

"It's nice to meet someone great." Dale stuck out his hand and Joe shook it.

"Finny's being nice. It's good to meet you." Dale gave a laugh before letting his hand go. Finny went to grab Sky from his stall. She brought him out to *oohs* and *ahhs* from Dale.

"He's really beautiful," Dale patted Sky's neck. "I'd love to see you ride him."

"We're breaking him now, so hopefully soon."

"Great, I'll look forward to it. I gotta head out to work. See you tomorrow."

"Bye, Dale. Thanks again for the ride."

Dale hurried off and Finny turned back to Joe.

"Dale wants to learn to ride. I told him I could teach him."

Joe nodded, his face slack and unreadable as he led Sky to the ring. Finny grabbed her helmet and followed him. After a leg up, Finny asked Sky to walk forward. He did so without hesitation.

"So far so good, right Joe?"

Joe nodded but looked away.

"Should I ask for a trot?" she suggested. Joe glanced at her then.

"How does he feel?"

"Okay, I guess."

Joe rubbed his chin and contemplated the horse. "He's been good, but I think he's starting to get bored, and he acts out when he's bored."

"Well, I'll give it a shot."

Finny asked for the first time for Sky to go faster, just into a slow trot. Sky jerked his body when Finny gave him a light nudge, then another. Finally a nudge and a cluck put Sky into a trot for one step before he threw a massive buck. All Finny saw was blue sky, ground, blue sky, ground before landing with a hard smack on her back. The world around her dimmed for a moment then snapped bright. Joe was by her side in an instant.

"Finny, are you okay?" Joe grabbed Finny's hand and held it in his.

Finny gasped for breath, the wind knocked out of her. Joe put his arm around her and helped her sit up.

"Yes . . . what happened?" Finny asked when she could speak. "I was on him and now . . ."

"He bucked you off. I'm so sorry, he gave no warning."

"I didn't feel any either. He was relaxed, then boom."

"Can you walk?" Joe asked, distraught.

"Oh yeah, I'm fine, just got my bell rung a little."

"Sit over here. I'm going to get on him." Joe led Finny to the side of the ring under a tree, out of the sun.

"Be careful, Joe." Finny realized she was going to see him ride for the first time.

With surprising agility and grace Joe swung up on Sky, not bothering with the stirrup. Finny was already impressed with just that. She adjusted herself against the post, trying to get more comfortable. Now that the shock was wearing off, several pockets of pain sprung up along her back and hip. Finny rubbed her backside and watched Joe walk Sky around the arena. She could tell right off he was a natural. On the back of a horse was where he belonged. Joe walked Sky in circles, patting his neck, telling him he was a good boy. Listening to Joe's soothing tones was working on Finny too. She was starting to relax.

Joe asked Sky for a trot, with leg and voice at the same time while in a tight turn. Sky responded and moved out at a trot. Joe did the best he could to keep Sky's mind occupied. He moved him in a figure eight pattern.

After the first fifteen seconds Joe felt Sky relax. He knew then Sky understood what he was supposed to do. Knowing he didn't have much time because Sky's attention span was so short, Joe gently pulled on the reins and asked the horse to come to a walk. Joe rode Sky to Finny and slid to the ground.

Finny, who was trying to be reasonable and rational, was having a hard time dealing with the fact that Joe was accepted by her horse and rode him so well after she had been instantly tossed to the dirt. She tried not to let her bruised ego show.

"Joe, you were amazing up there. Apparently he likes you." Finny let out a sigh and rubbed another sore spot.

"Remember, it doesn't have anything to do with like or not. He's easily annoyed and acts out. As soon as I gave him something to think about he was good to go."

"Thanks, Joe. That makes me feel better." Finny

struggled to get up. Joe offered her his hand, which she took.

"Finny, I'm sorry, I know I've said this a bunch of times but he doesn't act like a normal horse. He's going to be tough."

"But you think it's possible for him to be a safe riding horse, right?"

Joe looked sheepish and shrugged his shoulders. "I can't tell yet. He needs to deal with pressure better. And the fact he's so big and powerful makes it all the harder."

"Joe, I trust you completely so whatever you say goes."

"Okay, we'll just take it slow. Tomorrow I'll ride him first, then you get on."

"If he doesn't try to kill me it will be a great birthday present."

Finny and Joe walked to the Azure Hills sign. Joe was waiting with Finny until her mom came.

"How are you feeling?"

"Not bad. I'll be fine."

"Sorry."

"Joe, stop saying you're sorry—it's not your fault."

Joe nodded but still felt bad.

"So now that you're rolling in dough what are you

going to do? And if you say pay me back I'm gonna punch you."

Joe cracked a smile then a laugh.

"Thanks for the warnin'. I don't know, bank account first I guess."

"Vel said she'd help you get your birth certificate so you can get all set up."

"Yes, she did."

"I told you she was nice."

"Finny, she's the meanest woman I've ever met."

"What? Why?"

"She's making me go back to school. Said she won't help me get a driver's license unless I do. That's downright cruel."

Finny laughed, then grabbed her sore side. "Ow, ouch. Don't make me laugh."

A horn honked. Finny looked; her mom was coming fast.

"Oh boy, she's in a hurry. I'll see you tomorrow, Joe."

Beth screeched to a stop in front of the kids. She leaned down and lowered the passenger side window. "Hello, you must be Dale. It's so nice to meet the young man who was sweet enough to send flowers to my daughter."

"What flowers? Mom this is Joe, not Dale. My friend Joe."

"Oh, sorry. Let's go, Finny. Nice to meet you, Joe."

Beth had already looked away. Joe realized he wasn't interesting to Finny's mother since he wasn't flower-sending Dale.

"Sorry, Joe. My mom." Finny shrugged her shoulders, "I'll see you tomorrow, same time?" Joe nodded and turned away.

Joe stopped by the Silver Spur barn to check the horses. All the students had gone for the day and it was peaceful and quiet, just how he liked it. Joe walked over to one of the colts he was breaking and stroked its nose. The three-year-old warmblood blew on his shoulder and began to nibble his shirt. Joe gently removed his shirt from the young horse's mouth. He didn't have many clothes and needed to keep what he had in one piece. Since the young horse could no longer play, it turned away. Joe leaned his arm on the stall door and rested his cheek on his fist and watched the horses. After a few minutes he began to feel better. He wished he knew how Finny felt. He thought she liked him, but as more than a friend? Now that Dale was around, was it hopeless? He had no idea. If she did want to be more than friends, wouldn't she have said something by now? Elsa did, all the time. No question there.

"Joe, I didn't expect to see you here." It was Elsa. Joe closed his eyes and steadied himself. She made him nervous.

"I live and work here," Joe stated simply, no sarcasm intended.

"True. What are you doing here all by yourself?"

"Same as you I guess."

Elsa let out a giggle she hid behind her hand.

"Why so sad, Joe?"

"I'm not sad."

"For the record, you're a really bad liar."

Joe didn't respond, just turned his eyes back to the horses.

"I'm sorry Finny's going to the dance with Dale. She probably figured you didn't know how to dance."

Joe shot Elsa a quick wide-eyed look before he could stop himself.

"Oh gosh, you didn't know. I'm so sorry. I thought that was why you were sad."

"I gotta go, Elsa." Joe hurried out of the barn, Elsa on his heels.

"Joe, wait, let me help you. I can teach you to dance. You can show her that you learned just for her. It'd show her how much you care!"

Chapter Sixteen

Finny stared at the flowers Dale had sent. Her mom had put them in a vase. They were a gorgeous mixed bouquet. As soon as they walked in the door the interrogation was on. Dale this, Dale that, why didn't you tell me about Dale? The note on the flowers promised a corsage to match if she said yes to the dance.

"Dale Rutherford . . . Lance Rutherford's son, Lance Rutherford who owns this town? His son asked you to a dance? Finny, call him right now, the answer is yes."

"Mom, I don't want to go to the dance with him. I was getting up the nerve to ask Joe."

"Who's Joe?"

"Mom, you just met him tonight when you picked me up."

"Finny, honey, I'm sure Joe is nice but he's not a Rutherford. Call Dale, take Joe to the next dance."

"I don't have his number."

"It's here on the card."

"Seriously Mom, I want to go with Joe."

"Is this Joe your boyfriend?"

"No, just a friend."

Beth sat down next to Finny at the table.

"Sweetheart, call Dale. Go on the date. If it doesn't work out then go on a date with Joe. Trust me, Finny, you need to learn there's a big difference between the Joes and the Dales of the world."

The alarm rang. Finny woke to the realization that she was fifteen years old. After a quick stretch she got out of bed and went to the bathroom. Looking in the mirror she saw no difference. She thought she'd feel different, older, wiser, that life would be easier.

If anything, life was more complicated. She loved her mother and it would make her mother very happy if she went with Dale to the dance. Her mom was taking an interest in her again. Finny was lonely for a parent who paid attention to her. She groaned out loud. She didn't want to go with Dale; she wanted Joe. Finny thought about putting her foot down but worried her mom would be so disappointed she'd shut her out again, just like when her dad walked out. By the time Finny made it downstairs she was miserable.

"Surprise!" rang out from kitchen. Finny's sisters jumped up and down, hugged her, and said happy birthday no less than fourteen times. They gave her birthday drawings they had done just for her. She hugged them back, told them she loved them bunches, and proudly displayed the pictures on the fridge. Steven gave Finny a hug next and wished her a happy birthday. She was touched and happy he'd stayed home from work, knowing how busy he was with his new job. Beth smothered her daughter in a hug and a kiss, told her she was the most beautiful fifteen-year-old she'd ever seen, and that she was very proud of her. After that she told Finny to sit and served scrambled eggs and French toast, Finny's favorites. It was a morning she would never forget.

Once breakfast was finished Beth drove Finny to school. She wished her daughter a happy day and told her again to say yes to Dale. Finny kissed her mom, thanked her for the wonderful morning, got out, and made her way to class.

Finny was in a whirlwind. She'd disappoint her mom terribly if she didn't go to the dance with Dale. But she couldn't imagine going with anyone but Joe.

After biology class, Finny didn't see Dale at her locker. She found out he was home sick. She was sorry he was ill but relieved that it gave her another day to dodge the dance bullet. At lunch two girls came up to her. She knew they were cheerleaders and wildly popular but had never spoken to either one before.

"So we hear you're going to the dance with Dale?"

"Not sure yet." Finny, having no interest in the *in* crowd, brushed past them.

"Wait!" said one of the girls as she ran after Finny. "We were thinking of all going in and getting a limo, if you were interested." Finny searched their faces for sincerity. She couldn't tell and didn't care. Her sudden popularly was irritating. She had been the same person last year. Why hadn't she been good enough then?

"I'm sorry, not sure I'm even going. If I do, I'll let you know." Finny turned away again and made her way to class. Three more hours until Joe and Sky. She didn't think she'd make it.

The bell rang just before Finny lost her mind. She ran to the buses, only to be stopped by her mom who was waiting for her at the curb.

"Let's go, Finny. We got a cell phone to buy."

An hour and a half later, Finny was on her way to Azure Hills setting up her pink rhinestone-covered phone to play a cool ringtone. The only things that could make her birthday better would be seeing Joe and not getting bucked off of Sky. She couldn't wait.

"Thanks, Mom. You're the best. I'll see you at six!"

"Bye, baby." Finny gave her mom a kiss on the cheek and ran up the Azure Hills driveway. She saw Sky tacked and ready and Joe on the chair tipped back and waiting for her. When she got close she noticed a red ribbon on Sky's bridle. Then she noticed the bridle. It was a show bridle, a top-of-the-line expensive one. It was beautiful with its ornate stitching and it fit Sky perfectly.

"Joe, oh geez."

Joe smiled and dug at the dirt with his toe. "Happy birthday, Finny," he managed to say. Finny looked at the bridle. Joe could have bought just an average one for everyday use. But Joe, knowing Finny wanted a show-jumping horse, bought a show-jumping bridle as if to say, *I will make your dream come true.* Finny ran her fingers down the soft leather.

"So are you ready?" Joe said. Finny grabbed him in a hug. She didn't care if it was right or wrong, she held him tight. Joe was so special, so wonderful, she never wanted to let him go. He didn't tense up; in fact, she felt him relax as he wrapped his arms around her shoulders and hugged her back. It was the most warm, wonderful feeling in the world.

Sky nickered and shoved the pair apart with his big head, making them both laugh.

"I think he was getting bored," Finny reasoned.

"I think he was gettin' jealous," Joe said.

Finny hugged Sky, then told Joe to hug him too because she wasn't sure who he liked better. Joe laughed again and gave Sky a hug.

Once mounted, Joe and Sky walked around the arena. The horse responded and moved beautifully off his leg. After a few minutes Joe asked for a trot. Again, right off the leg, smooth and steady. Joe asked for a few transitions and was pleased with Sky's behavior. He rode over to Finny and slid to the ground. A moment later he legged Finny up on Sky and led her once around the ring. Finny tentatively asked her horse to walk forward. Sky listened.

"Finny, be bold and take charge when you're on his back."

"Okay." Finny gave him a little kick and asked him to trot. She got about ten steps before he stopped, humped his back, and threw a buck. Not as hard as the first one, but still enough to take Finny to the dirt. Once she was on the ground Sky came to her, blew in her face, and then ran to the other side of the arena.

"Oh no, not again! Joe, he hates me."

Joe was instantly at her side, helping her up.

"No, unfortunately it's the opposite. You're like a plaything to him. He likes you, but on his terms."

"So what does that mean?"

"We got to keep trying. I'll get on him again." Joe jumped back on Sky and worked him for a solid five minutes.

"I'm gonna see what he does when I make him aggravated. I'm not gonna hurt him, I'm just gonna work him 'til he's tired or bored." Joe rode for a solid twenty minutes. Sky was covered in sweat but still going strong. Not getting any negative reaction, Joe upped it a notch. He asked for a canter. Sky took two canter steps before bolting out of control around the arena. Joe sat deep in the saddle and rode it out. He knew that as long as he didn't panic he could ride out a bolt. Joe hauled on the reins but to no avail. If Sky even felt it, he didn't care. Joe was amazed by the horse's power and strength. The mustangs and quarter horses he was used to were half the size of this animal, and Sky felt at least ten times stronger. Using both hands, Joe was able to yank the right rein and turn Sky's head into the fence. That finally got his attention enough to slow him down. Once stopped, Sky let out a huge buck. Joe, who had ridden rodeo broncs for years, just barely held on. Now covered with sweat and totally out of breath, Joe slid down from the horse and took off his hat. He used his shirtsleeve to dry his forehead, walked over to Finny, handed her the reins, and fell in the grass exhausted.

"I'll cool him out and put him away, Joe. If you're not back on your feet by then, I'll call nine-one-one."

Through panting breaths Joe said, "It's too late." Finny laughed at his melodramatics.

"If we get this one broke, we can break anything. Lions, tigers, bears, anything," Joe called after her.

By the time Sky was hosed off and put in his stall, Joe was back on his feet. Finny was just closing the barn door when she heard her mother's car horn.

"Uh, Joe, what do you think about getting a cell phone?"

"Never thought about it."

"I . . . sometimes, need, or would like to talk to you but can't until I see you . . . and the business, if you had phone, people could call you directly instead of having to go through Vel."

"Okay." The horn honked three more times.

"Great, we'll get you one Saturday! I'll see you tomorrow." Finny dashed off toward her mother's car.

"Hi, Mom. Where are we going?" Finny asked, when they turned away from home.

"To a birthday dinner for a very special daughter." Finny smiled. She knew her mom was up to something. She could see it on her face.

It was the shock of a lifetime. Her father was there with Linda and their kids. It was the first time they all were together in one place, ever. Expecting the worst, Finny found her parents and stepparents at ease in each other's company and the four little kids fell into an instant friendship. Finny, for the first time in a long time, felt there was hope.

It was her birthday, so Beth couldn't say no when Finny wanted to run to Silver Spur with a piece of birthday cake for Joe.

"Be quick," Beth said as Finny dashed out of the car and around the barn. Elsa's car was parked in Joe's drive. Finny looked at her watch—it was almost nine. She stood and stared, paralyzed with dread for five long minutes, positive she was going to be sick.

This was why he never made the next move. He'd fallen for Elsa. It was crystal clear now. He only acted like a friend because that was all he was. Finny went to the side of the trailer and peeked into a window from a distance. She saw them standing in each other's arms. The piece of cake dropped to the ground. Finny bolted back to the car, said nothing to her mother, and made it home just in time to throw up.

Chapter Seventeen

———

THE DAY WAS BRIGHT AND SUNNY BUT TO FINNY it was socked in. A fog of misery followed her every move. First period dragged on forever and she wasn't sure she heard a word her teacher said. Biology was next . . . Dale was next. She'd have to face him now; he couldn't be sick forever. And he wasn't. He was walking down the hall toward her. Finny opened her locker.

"Hi, Finny."

"Hey, Dale."

"You okay?"

Finny shrugged her shoulders.

"Are you getting sick?"

Finny shook her head.

"So, I hate to be a pest but the dance is Friday . . . am I picking you up?"

"Sure." Finny gave him a small smile.

Dale frowned. "I'm looking forward to it. It'll be a blast."

"Good, I could use some fun."

It felt like it took several years but the school day finally ended. Finny, not wanting to deal with Dale, hid till he left and then went to the buses.

Once at Azure Hills she found Joe waiting as he usually did. He was a man of his word, after all. Finny made her way toward Joe, flipping up her phone to check her message from her mother.

"Wow, you got a phone!"

"For my birthday." She handed it to him.

"Perfect! When I get mine we can talk whenever."

We? Finny thought. Elsa wouldn't tolerate any *we* when it came to Joe. It would only be a matter of time before she broke up their friendship. All last night and all day Finny had struggled to get it okay in her head. After all, her life's ambition was not to be a stupid suffering-after-a-boy girl.

She'd convinced herself she wanted it that way because she was more evolved, more enlightened, but the truth was, she was just a big chicken. She didn't want her feelings kicked around and to suffer heartache. Watching her mom's downhill spiral after her dad left had been more than instructive; it had been devastating.

Finny watched Joe as he checked out the phone. Maybe once they were together for a while and Elsa got what she wanted, she'd get bored and kick him to the curb. Maybe then, Joe would want her.

"Congratulations," Joe said, all smiles as he handed the phone back. Finny did her best to smile back. She'd just take things day by day. She wondered when Joe would break the Elsa news. She was sure he was hesitating because of their history. Sooner or later, he'd have to.

"You ready for Sky?"

"Who do you think should go first?"

"I lunged him, took some of his energy down, so go ahead and try."

"Okay." Finny stroked Sky's long mahogany neck and spoke soothing words. Sky pinned his ears and ground his bit hard between his teeth.

"Joe, he's already mad and I haven't even gotten on him yet."

"I see that. Let me try." Joe moved into position and Sky stomped his foot to show his displeasure.

"I'm going to take him to the arena and lunge him again." Joe walked him over and before they even got to the middle of the arena Sky tried to bolt. Joe was able to stop him thanks to the line through his bit. Sky spun right to face Joe and dug at the ground with his hoof, grunting with every strike.

"Come on, Sky, get going." Joe asked the horse to circle around him. Sky tried again to pull away. Joe finally got the horse under control and going. It was at an all-out gallop in a circle around him, but at least he was moving.

Twenty minutes Sky ran without stopping. Finny wondered what that translated into mile-wise. Sky, head down and pouring sweat, huffed and puffed like a freight train. Joe pulled Sky to a stop, quickly unhooked the lunge line, and swung up into the saddle as Sky was still battling for air. Joe patted him and kept him walking so his muscles wouldn't cramp.

Although Sky was dead tired his ears stayed pinned down and his tail swished periodically.

"How does he feel, Joe?"

"Tense through his back, mad."

"He looks mad."

"I'm going to try a trot." Joe nudged him forward with his heels. Sky instantly kicked out at the pressure of Joe's leg. Joe nudged him again and asked for a trot. Sky humped his back, then shot up in the air in a wild rear. Joe, caught off guard, grabbed Sky's mane and held on. Sky dropped to the ground and bolted, bucking, twisting, anything he could do to dislodge his rider. Joe pulled him into a tight circle trying to get the big horse under control. Sky spun, then stopped suddenly as if frozen. Then, in a fit of rage, he threw himself over backward.

"Joe!" Finny ran into the arena. Joe was trapped beneath Sky, the horse's weight crushing his right leg. Finny grabbed the bridle and pulled, desperate to get Sky up. Joe pushed against Sky's back in a fruitless effort to get the more than half-ton animal off his leg.

"Sky, come on, get up." Finny yanked again. Sky, dull and sullen, refused to move. Joe finally gasped and fell back to the ground, the pain overcoming him. Finny yanked again and again, then ran out of the arena and grabbed a whip. She lashed Sky across the hindquarters. She knew how he'd react and she was right. He bolted up, then spun and came at her. Expecting this, Finny jumped out of the way, just missing being bowled over. Sky kept going, across the ring, then jumped out, tore down the property line, and leapt over the fence into Silver Spur and disappeared out of sight.

"Joe, are you okay? Your leg, that's your bad leg." Joe, pale and panting, got up to his elbows, looked at Finny, then closed his eyes, breathing like he'd run a marathon. "Joe, I'm so sorry. Please tell me you're okay."

He sat up and gingerly put his hand on his knee.

"I'm okay, Finny. I don't know what's wrong. He's so angry. I've never come across a horse like this." Joe lay back on the dirt and put his hands over his eyes.

"Stay put. I'm going to grab your crutches—they're still in the tack room. We've got to ice your knee." Joe nodded without removing his hands from his face.

Finny was back in a minute with the crutches and a cup of water. Joe was sitting up by the time she arrived. Using the crutches, he got up, then drank the water. They made their way to the tack room and Joe sat in the chair. Finny ran to Vel's house and grabbed an ice pack. Joe rubbed his knee, then bent and straightened it without pain.

"If it was broken, you wouldn't be able to do that."

Joe put the ice pack on his knee. "You're right. It just feels a little funny, doesn't really hurt."

"Thank God. Joe will you be okay here? I better get Sky."

"Yeah, I'll be fine."

Finny ran all the way to Silver Spur. She didn't even want to think what damage Sky could be inflicting right now. Once at the ring, Finny was surprised to find it empty. This was a normal lesson time for the advanced students. She also noticed the barn doors were closed.

A moment later the door slid open a crack and Clara peeked out. "Finny, please get that crazy horse of yours out of here."

"Where is he?"

"I don't know. He jumped into the ring, started to herd all the horses in the lesson. Jeff and Barbara ran to catch him. He charged them, then jumped over them and out of the arena. He ran halfway down the property, then turned and was coming back at us full speed. We all took cover in the barn."

"I don't see him anywhere."

"Please go find him, and get him out of here!"

"I'll get him. I'm so sorry!" Finny dashed to the side of the barn. Sky was nowhere to be found, until she heard a bang and a crash. She closed her eyes and prayed, *Please don't be where I think you are.* Finny ran to the feed room. The wooden steps to the door were broken, not meant for a now fourteen-hundred-pound horse. The door was splintered and hanging from one hinge. Sky was munching away on the bags of sweet feed that had just been delivered. Not happy with just one, Sky had torn all six bags before choosing which one to eat.

"Oh, Sky." The sound of Finny's voice made the horse turn and look in her direction. Sky let out an earsplitting neigh and quickly trotted out of the feed room and jumped down the broken stairs. He went right up to Finny and nuzzled her cheek and blew warm breath in her ear. Finny sadly patted his head and took the reins, amazed the bridle was still in one piece. She poked her head into the barn and told everyone it was all clear. Finny apologized at least fifteen more times and headed back to Azure Hills.

Once back, she led Sky to his stall. When Sky spotted Joe he let out a neigh and dragged Finny over to him. Sky immediately started rubbing his head on Joe, all but knocking him from the chair.

"Okay, Sky, I'm not a scratching post. Behave." Sky nuzzled Joe's uplifted hand. Joe gave Sky a rub behind the ear before Finny put him away.

"You're not going to believe what he did. I don't know what's going to happen. I'm pretty much dead."

"Uh oh, what?"

"He ran over, herded the horses in the lesson. Jumped over Jeff and Barbara when they tried to stop him. Jumped out of the ring, tore around the property, charged back to the ring, causing everyone to dash to the barn and hide. Then he goes to the back, walks up the steps to the feed room, destroying them, busts open the door, tears up bags of feed, then eats. That's what he was doing when I found him." Joe, who had put his hand over his mouth when Finny began the tale, now was using both hands, trying desperately not to laugh.

"Oh, glad you think it's funny, since it's only me who will be banned for life."

"I'm sorry, it's not funny." Joe just managed to get out before breaking out in hysterics. Finny pinched the bridge of her nose trying not to join him. She couldn't help it—she laughed too.

"Joe, you should have seen Clara's face. All of them, hiding from a horse." The two laughed until their sides stitched.

"Joe, let's get you home, since it's the last time I'll be allowed on the property."

"No, that's not going to happen."

They made their way toward Silver Spur. At the fence line, Finny paused and said, "I hope you're right, but honestly, this may be the final straw."

"No way. If they ban you, I'll quit."

"You would? You'd quit?"

"Of course. I wouldn't stand for them treating you like that."

"Thanks, Joe. That's really sweet."

Joe nodded—it went without saying. She realized, as much as she loved him, losing him as a friend would be unthinkable. Finny was determined just to deal with it when he and Elsa became a public thing. She could do that for a friend, especially someone as special as Joe.

"Thanks, Finny. I'll see you tomorrow."

"Oh, uh . . . I won't be here tomorrow." Finny felt like a pile of bricks had landed on her. The stupid dance she'd wanted to go to with him so badly was tomorrow. Standing there now, with Joe, it was painful to think about. "I got something to do." Lousy excuse, but it was the best she could come up with.

"Oh, okay." Joe looked a bit surprised. "Saturday then."

Finny wanted him to know she was his friend no matter what. Before she lost the nerve she blurted out, "Joe, just so you know, I'm totally cool with you and Elsa, I swear." Finny turned and hurried off, proud of herself for doing it even if it was the biggest lie she'd ever told.

Chapter Eighteen

JOE MADE HIS WAY TO THE BACK OF THE BARN, confused about what Finny meant about Elsa. That thought flew from his brain when he saw Sky's path of destruction. Trying not to limp on an increasingly sore leg, Joe gathered the tools he'd need to fix the damage. Within the hour the broken stair boards were replaced and the feed room door was back on, as well as the feed scooped up and put into bins.

Joe was just about to start the last coat of paint on the repaired steps when he heard Elsa's voice calling his name. He let out a groan and hoped she wouldn't look behind the barn. Joe painted as fast as he could. He wanted to get done so he could sneak to his trailer without her seeing him. At least a hurt leg would be a good excuse to avoid another nightmare of a dance lesson.

"There you are!"

"Hey, Elsa."

"I see you're covering her tracks. You're a nice friend all things considered."

"I'm just fixing what's broke, and for the record Sky dumped me, which is why he got loose. This wasn't Finny's fault."

"Good luck convincing Jeff. I think her days here are done."

"Let me know if that's so, because that'll be my last day too."

"Don't say that." Elsa sat on the still solid part of the porch and put her hand on Joe's shoulder. "This job is very important for you. It's good for your reputation as a horse trainer and as a professional." Joe didn't answer as he continued to paint.

"You're so tense." Elsa began kneading the tight muscle in his shoulder.

"Elsa, please, I gotta finish painting."

"Why are you so loyal to her? You know she's dating Dale. They're going to the school dance tomorrow night. She's made her choice. It's time you realized that and moved on." Joe stopped what he was doing and stood.

"She is? She's going to a dance with him *tomorrow*?"

"Yes, Joe, I've been trying to tell you." Elsa stepped in front of him and laid her hand on his chest, "Let me help you move on." Running her hand through his hair, Elsa attempted to draw Joe into a kiss. Caught by surprise, he pulled away.

"Elsa, what are you doing?"

"What do you think? Why are you so hung up on her? She loves someone else. She doesn't want you. You are either incredibly blind or completely stupid. On top of that I'm here for you and you just push me away. Finny's right, you're not good enough as a horse trainer or a boyfriend!"

The dress was spectacular. Her makeup was perfect and Finny's styled hair shimmered in the light. Finny thought to herself she'd never looked this good, this grown up, or felt this miserable. She kept a happy face on for her mom, who was beside herself with joy. Her once socially awkward wallflower of a daughter was coming out of her shell and dating the most handsome, sought-after boy in school. Dale arrived right on time and her mom and Steven took an embarrassing number of pictures. They proceeded to tell Dale repeatedly how thrilled they were that Finny and he were going to the dance. Finny finally had to pry her mother off of Dale's arm so they could go.

Once in the car, Finny said, "Sorry, Dale, that was mortifying."

Dale laughed and shook his head. "Your parents are super nice."

"Glad someone thinks so." Dale laughed again.

"So, is this your first dance?"

"Yep, first ever."

"I know you're going to have fun. And I know I said it already but you look amazing."

"Thanks, Dale, you're very sweet."

The remainder of the drive was quiet. Dale pulled up, parked, then went to open Finny's door.

"Thank you." Finny looked up at the fancy decorations surrounding the door. She saw a bunch of her classmates going in and out. It was weird seeing them all dressed up. Finny looked at Dale. He had a somber expression on his handsome face.

"What's wrong?" Finny asked.

"I'm not sure. You look like you're about to head into a funeral."

"Oh, do I? I'm sorry . . . got a lot on my mind."

"Finny, can we just sit outside for a minute? I want to ask you something."

They sat on the bench outside the gym door. Their fellow classmates said hello as they came and went. Dale cleared his throat before he began. "I've dated some and had a serious girlfriend once for a summer . . . and, well, what I'm trying to say is . . ." Dale huffed out a breath. "Elsa said you had a mad crush on me and really wanted to go out. I always thought you were cute, but had no idea you liked me. So, figuring you were shy, I made the first move. The thing is, I kinda don't get that you-have-a-mad-crush-on-me vibe from you."

"Oh God, Dale. I'm so sorry. You're a great guy, but Elsa's a big trouble-making liar." Finny slumped back on the bench, feeling ill. "I'm so sorry. You're really awesome, it's just . . . I . . ."

"Like someone else." Dale finished. Finny looked at him, bit her lip, and nodded. Dale let out a sigh and leaned back on the bench. "Well that makes me feel better. I thought I was losing my mojo," Dale said with a smile.

Finny put her hand over her mouth and laughed.

"That'd never happen, Dale."

"So I'm guessing it's Joe, the guy I met at the ranch." Finny nodded. "And, since Elsa played me like a puppet, I'm guessing she likes this Joe too." Finny nodded again.

"Wow, he must have super mojo."

Finny laughed even harder.

"So does Joe know how you feel?"

Finny shrugged her shoulders. "I think he might have fallen for Elsa."

"So you don't know?"

"Not really."

"Well, it's up to you. If you would like to dance I'm yours for the evening, but if Elsa has worked Joe, like she worked me, I think you better go talk to him."

Chapter Nineteen

———

IT WAS THE RUN, THE ALL-OUT, GO-FOR-BROKE, don't-stop-till-you're-almost-dead run. Joe was sure of it. He kicked Sky on. The horse flew across the ground, bathed in the eerie blue hue of the rising moon. Joe knew Sky had spent almost twelve years in horse isolation, half starved with no care. He was a horse filled with anger and confusion with a lifetime of frustration to get out of his system.

Finny sitting with Dale on the bench outside the dance tortured Joe's thoughts. All along, Elsa had been right.

Out of desperation, Joe had taken the ranch truck and driven to the high school. He had to see for himself, had to know for sure. He didn't have a license yet, but didn't care. He'd been driving since he was thirteen.

She was there, shining like a goddess in her beautiful dress, with Dale by her side. It was more than Joe's heart could take.

After a few miles, Sky no longer needing Joe's urging. The horse thundered over the ground out of pure need, his spirit soaring. Joe knew he had to make Sky better; he had to keep his promise. If he did, then maybe there was a chance she could love him.

At the base of the mountain Joe felt the change, in Sky's stride or his mind, he wasn't sure, but the horse switched on. Sky ran like he was bred to. It took all Joe had to stay on. Miles were disappearing in minutes but Sky wasn't tiring. If anything, this new adventure was pounding adrenaline through his veins, feeding the will to go on. The higher they went, the harder the trails were to negotiate, but Sky had a sense all his own. Joe wasn't sure the horse would listen if he tried to guide him. The underbrush was thick, but what Sky couldn't run through he jumped over, almost frantic as if his life depended on getting to the top of the mountain.

Joe didn't know how long they'd been running, but he felt that a lifetime of misery lay behind in the dust and hoofprints they left. In his mind, Joe needed the run as badly as Sky, but his body was human and was wearing out. He had to slow the horse down and prayed Sky would listen. With all his strength Joe pulled on the reins. He leaned back using his body's weight, but it was useless. Sky bore down hard on the bit, yanking Joe to his neck, then burst forward. Joe hung on, hoping for enough stamina to ride it out. He buried his face in Sky's mane to avoid the overhanging branches that constantly whipped him as they sped by. Sweat and foam poured from Sky's body, making the reins almost too slippery to hold. Joe laced his fingers through Sky's thick mane for a better grip. Exhaustion was taking over. If he didn't stop soon, he'd fall, and at the speed they were going he didn't know if he'd survive it.

Joe began to talk to Sky, telling him he had to slow down, had to stop. Demanding anything of this horse didn't work. He'd have to ask Sky. Joe kept talking, telling him it was okay to stop now. They were easily halfway up the mountain. Joe watched Sky's ear flick back when he felt it, the slightest hint of Sky easing. Joe told him *whoa* and hauled back on the reins. It helped; Sky was listening. He broke stride. Another hard pull and Joe cut his speed to half. One more pull and Sky jerked to a sudden stop. Joe collapsed on Sky's neck before rolling to the ground in a tangle of underbrush. Joe lay there, exhausted, gasping for air, his knee on fire. The big horse hovered over him blowing warm breath in his face. Above Sky, the mass of stars burned bright and it was beautiful.

Dale drove Finny to Silver Spur and wished her luck. Finny told him how much she appreciated everything.

She hopped out of his car and ran to Joe's trailer. This was it, she was going to spill her guts. If he confessed his feelings for Elsa, at least she'd have tried. Dale was right—she wasn't going to give up without a fight. Finny knocked loudly on Joe's door—no answer. Frustrated, she checked the windows. No sign of Joe. Finally, she tried the door and found it unlocked. She called his name. Nothing. He wasn't there.

Her stomach seized when she realized that he must be with Elsa. All the air felt sucked out of her as she wandered across the field to Azure Hills. She needed to at least see Sky. Finny leaned into his stall and called to him. The stall was empty. The contrast of a white folded piece of paper against the dark of Sky's feeder drew her attention. She hurried into the stall to retrieve it.

> *Finny,*
> *I think I know why Sky acts out. I'm not sure it will work but I'm going to try. You deserve a great horse. I'll be back as soon as I can. I'm sorry I let you down. You looked like a princess in your dress tonight. Please give me one more chance.*
> *Joe*

Finny grabbed the note to her chest. She read it again. Tears streamed down her cheeks unabated. She ran to the end of the property and looked to the distant mountain. She knew Joe was there; she felt it. He'd go to what he knew. Finny scanned the dark mountain's face, visible thanks to the brilliant moon. She trusted Joe and his ability completely, but Sky was a wild card that had almost killed him.

Finny felt sick with dread. She should tell someone. What if Joe was up there hurt? No, she reasoned, he can do anything. He's proven that time and time again. If Joe said he'd be back, he'd be back, no question. Finny knew without a doubt he loved her. This was his way of telling her. Not with a hug or a word but with keeping a promise no matter the cost.

Chapter Twenty

———

J OE WOKE TO A FACE IN THE SUN AND A BODY FULL of aches and pains. He sat up and stretched the kinks out of almost every muscle he had.

Sky stood a few feet away grazing on the plentiful grass in the clearing. Joe looked him over. He was covered in dried sweat but was still in one piece. Of all the breakneck back-alley races Joe had run, none compared to this one. Sky had power and speed beyond belief.

Pain shot through Joe's leg when he tried standing, driving him back to the ground. He rubbed his knee and tried again, using his good leg, and got to his feet. Joe's head swam when he took his first step. After a minute of leaning on a tree he took another step toward the horse and the water pouch he'd attached to the saddle. Normally he wouldn't have bothered to bring water, but this was California, and water was scarce. His right leg felt like lead as he made his way toward Sky. He rubbed it again. The muscle was beginning to relax, making walking more possible.

"Hey, Sky. Good boy." Joe gave the horse a pat and took the water pouch. He drank half the bag before offering the rest to Sky. The big horse finished up the water. Joe surveyed the area; he had no idea where he was. He'd never expected Sky to go so far so fast. Joe knew he had been right. Sky needed the run, needed the freedom. Today would be pivotal. Sky had to want to work with people for Finny to have any chance of a riding horse. A horse with this much heart needed a purpose. Joe had ridden enough champion horses to know they made themselves great because they wanted it.

Ten miles was Joe's guess, to the top of the mountain. Doing the best he could not to hurt his leg, Joe mounted Sky. He urged him to walk forward. Sky pawed the ground once and walked on. He felt like a horse in a starting gate, ready to bolt. Joe tested his leg by standing in the stirrup. It wasn't too bad. He said a silent prayer and hoped he and his knee would hold up. After a deep breath Joe urged Sky into a canter. He pointed the horse up the trail and let the reins loose. If Sky wanted to all-out run it was up to him. And run Sky did.

It was like stepping into another world when Joe and Sky broke through the cloudbank and crested the mountaintop. Joe was made dizzy by the vastness around him, by the beauty of the brilliant blue sky. He heard an eagle cry, and, to his amazement, it soared beneath him, its giant wingspan keeping it aloft on the warm upswelling current. Joe turned his face to the sun and filled his lungs with the crisp, pure air, letting it energize his body and spirit.

He stared into the distance, not comprehending what his eyes saw. It surely was the edge of the earth. Joe realized that for the first time in his life, he was looking at the ocean. It was a moment most spiritual. Joe understood fully why his Indian ancestors worshiped nature. The proof was all around him. He felt one with the earth and part of the sky. He knew he was halfway to heaven when he closed his eyes and prayed to his parents, prayed to the earth below, the sky above, and to God who was everywhere. His prayer was simple: *Help him be strong and show him the way.* That's all he needed.

Finny packed up what tack and supplies she had stored in the Silver Spur tack room. Leaving seemed surreal. She was surprised she didn't feel as sad as she thought she would. She'd learned a lot in her four years here. Not all about riding. She'd learned about people too, the good and the bad.

Barbara was the one who had broken the news with tears in her eyes. Finny felt sorry the job of kicking her out had been dumped on Barbara. The truth of it was, Finny was relieved. Four years of Elsa torment had gotten old. Now with Joe in the mix, it had become too intense.

Finny put her stuff in the bed of Vel's truck, then Vel drove her up to Joe's trailer. She dreaded breaking the news to him. Elsa wanted them both gone, and Elsa got her way.

Finny and Vel moved around Joe's trailer gathering his things. It was painful remembering how happy he'd been when he moved in, how badly he'd wanted a home. Joe hadn't lied when she'd asked if he'd run from home, because his home had been long gone by the time he ran.

It only took fifteen minutes and one box to pack all Joe's belongings. Finny looked at the nice furniture that filled the trailer. Elsa had done all this just to exert control. Did money do that to a person, or would she have found another way had she been poor? It made no sense.

Once everything was packed Finny let out a deep

breath and got in the truck. She mentally said good-bye to what had been her second home as Vel pulled away. She'd hoped Jeff would be there to wish her well, but for whatever reason, he wasn't.

Back at Azure Hills, Vel parked her truck, took the box of Joe's stuff, and went inside to put it in the spare room. Finny went through the back of the property to the base of the mountain where she'd been waiting ever since she found Joe's note, only leaving to pick up their things from Silver Spur.

The tears were real when she called her mom, but they were for Joe, not a sick horse Finny convinced her mother she needed to stay overnight with at Azure Hills. She'd also had to tell her mother the dance was fun, rebuffing her mother's many questions.

The guilt began to take its toll on Finny. The longer she kept Joe and Sky secret the more lies she told.

Chapter Twenty-One

———

I T WAS A DIFFERENT HORSE UNDERNEATH HIM. JOE felt it in every step Sky took. He felt it in the way the horse breathed, in the calm, steady energy that flowed through him. Sky had let go. The adrenaline surge pushed out the anxiety. The gallons of sweat washed out the anger. Joe was able to direct Sky, now content enough to listen, down the mountain.

The wild out-of-control ride up had left Joe unsure as to where they were, but he knew the horse's natural instinct would guide them home.

Once in a clearing, Joe looked off to see if he could spot the town at the base of the mountain, but the earth below lay blanketed in mist, so again, it was up to Sky.

Moving through the cloudbanks made everything dreamlike. A little bit of heaven on earth, just like Finny said. And now, thanks to her, Joe could see it. He wished she were there with him. He pictured her eyes wide with wonder, her beautiful face lit up. Joe realized now he lived for those moments.

Sky continued on, diliger.tly picking the route. There was a good horse under him and Joe knew Sky was a horse that would let Finny live her dreams. He was happy; if nothing else at least he had done that for her. Joe wondered what she was thinking. He hoped she wasn't mad. He had taken her horse without asking. It was impulsive and Joe typically wasn't impulsive. It had been seeing Dale with Finny that had driven him to the desperate act. He contemplated what to do if Finny was truly in love with Dale. He'd already had so much heartache in his life, he didn't think he could take a new round of it. He'd have to leave. It was a painful revelation, but he would have no choice.

A touch of cold tickled Finny's shoulders. The sun had dropped past the horizon, its last rays burning the clouds, leaving long shadows. Finny gazed longingly up the mountain; she'd been watching and waiting for almost twenty-four hours.

The last of the light was quickly fading. Tears began to well in her eyes. Finny, angry with herself for being so blind, had been waiting for Joe to say it even though he'd shown her in a hundred different ways how he felt.

Now, because of her, he was up there on that formidable mountain, maybe hurt or in trouble.

The tree line, thick and beautiful, showed no signs of horse or rider. Finny's insides twisted. He said he'd be back. If she called for help, she'd break his trust or, worse, have him sent back to a life of misery with his uncle. Either one would be unforgivable. Finny closed her eyes. Joe had never let her down. She'd count to ten and he'd be there, coming back to her safe. With a prayer she began her count, giving several seconds between each number. When she finally whispered ten, she willed herself to open her eyes. Joe and Sky broke through the trees. Her heart stopped. Not sure she wasn't seeing things, Finny rubbed her eyes hard, forcing the tears from them. Joe was there, real, solid, and safe.

Finny made her way toward them through the tall grass. She saw Sky sweaty, dirty, happy, and healthy. Without a word Joe slipped off the horse. Finny, too choked up to speak and hardly able to breathe, reached up, touched his face, then kissed him softly on the lips. Joe drew Finny to him and held her tight. He took her face with both hands and kissed her again and again and again. Finny reveled in his warmth, in the feel of his arms around her. In how holding him, kissing him, and now loving him felt like the first right thing she had ever done.

Chapter Twenty-Two

E ARLY THE NEXT MORNING, SIDE BY SIDE, FINNY and Joe sat at Vel's kitchen table. Their clasped hands rested on the tabletop. Vel got up from her chair and offered to make hot chocolate. It did her heart good seeing the kids she'd grown to care for so happy. "Joe, how's the young horse here doing?"

"Jenna's going great, gentle as they come. Thanks to her, at least I'm not penniless."

"On that note, Joe, I expect you to stay here and I don't want you to argue or fuss about it. You work so hard here you've earned a place to live."

"Are you sure?"

"Absolutely."

"Thank you." Joe tried to smile, but losing his job and his own home still stung.

"I think you should do some advertising, like flyers at the feed store, for a start," Vel suggested.

"I can do that. If I get two more horses that's more than I'd make in a month at Silver Spur anyway. Maybe this was for the best."

"I think so too, for both of us," Finny said. "Unfortunately, now that Sky has come around, I don't have a jumping trainer."

"Yes you do," Vel said as she put the steaming cups of cocoa down on the table.

"What do you mean?"

Vel left the room and came back with photo albums and spread them out in front of the pair.

Finny sipped her cocoa and opened the first book. Picture after picture of Vel in the show ring, winning competition after competition. The next book was of all the magazine covers featuring Vel and her horses, and the articles written about them. The next book was full of Vel's numerous trainer awards. Finny saw they spanned over twenty-five years. She was dumbstruck. She looked up at Vel, sweet unassuming Vel, who ten years ago had been named trainer of the year for the third consecutive year. Something Jeff Hastings had never achieved.

"Oh, wow, you trained and competed show jumpers nationally?" Finny asked Vel with awe.

"Sure did."

"I'm stunned. I never knew. How come you aren't still training?"

Vel let out a contemplative breath. The answer was long and complicated.

"In a nutshell, I got into the sport because I loved horses. . . . They saved my life and made my dreams come true. It was time to pay them back."

Now that Vel was on board and Sky was ready, it was time to get serious. Vel asked Joe to start bringing the old jumps out from behind the barn. They needed to be repaired and repainted to be useful again. After cutting through the mass of weeds, Joe found a pile of thirty jump poles. Next to the poles was a flat tire. Joe had moved a dozen poles and cleared more weeds before he saw that attached to the flat tire was a pickup truck. After clearing more weeds, Joe discovered it was a 1951 Ford just like the one his dad had owned and so loved. With a shaky hand, Joe ran his fingers along the giant fenders, then down the hood. He couldn't tell what color it had been since the paint had long been replaced by primer and rust. Using the bottom of his shirt, Joe rubbed the dirt off the driver's side window and saw it was a manual, just like his dad's, and the interior was in good shape considering its age. Joe all but cried when he saw the unique wooden bed. The truck was a classic. Joe, forgetting the jumps, ran to Vel.

"Vel, you have a Fifty-one Ford behind the barn!" Joe told her, figuring she couldn't have known since it was covered in weeds and abandoned.

"Oh, yeah, that was my dad's old truck. Hasn't run in years."

"Why not?" Joe asked, beside himself with building excitement.

"I don't know. Forgot about it, to tell you the truth."

"You did?" Joe fought down the urge to say, *Are you insane?*

"Well, yeah. Joe, if you like the truck? You can have it."

Positive he was having a heart attack, Joe steadied his breathing.

"You can't mean it."

"I can and I do. Joe, you need to sit down, you've gone pale."

"You kidding? I've never been better. Vel, are you sure?"

"Of course I'm sure." Joe grabbed Vel in a bear hug, lifting her off her feet.

"Thank you so much! When I get it running then I can help out even more around here and maybe get a horse trailer. Fin-ny!" Joe hollered, then disappeared around the barn.

Vel, a bit shocked by Joe's uncharacteristic exuberance, couldn't help but laugh. Seeing him so happy was a very nice thing.

Despite the time Joe dedicated to his new old truck, working with Finny and Sky, and training his client's horse, he still managed to get the arena filled with brightly painted, newly fixed jumps of assorted types and colors within a few weeks.

Vel entered the arena just as Joe was setting the line to a six-stride.

"This arena looks even better than Silver Spur's main ring, Joe." Vel admired the angular coop, the artificial brick wall, the green-topped half-round. She was delighted to see the "Liverpool," complete with a blue tarp beneath it to look like water—all the obstacles Sky would eventually face in a show ring.

"That's what we need, right, to train Sky to be a show jumper?" Joe pushed his hat back and used his sleeve to dry his forehead.

"Joe, seriously, this is amazing. I've got to tell you, it's fun to be doing this again. Finny is a very talented rider. She could go far if Sky turns out to be as talented as we think he is."

"I hope so, Vel. I want her to be happy."

Vel gave Joe a smile. "She is happy, Joe, very happy."

A contented smile crossed Joe's face.

"Speaking of happiness, how're the night classes working out?"

"It's okay. Just mild torture."

Vel chuckled.

Finny appeared with Sky. She was mounted and ready for her lesson with Vel.

"Vel," Joe said. "Sky loves to jump. I still can't believe how quickly he took to it. While warming him up do things that keep him guessing a little. And jump as soon as you can."

"Will do, Joe. Thanks."

Finny began her warm-up. Sky felt relaxed and was listening well to her aids. After executing several transitions and circles to get Sky limber, she felt he was ready to jump.

"Go trot the crossrail, Finny."

She nodded and made her approach. Sky trotted up and stepped over, landing in a canter. He gave a playful toss of the head but that was it.

"Do that a couple more times, then canter the near line in a six."

Finny did as instructed. Sky, light and soft, cantered the jumps with six strides between them.

"Finny, collect him up and now do the line in seven." Finny asked for a shorter stride and Sky shifted his weight more to his hindquarters and put in seven even strides with no problem.

"Finny, Joe, I know he's still green, but I think he's ready to go to his first show. We need to see how he does in a strange place. We could take him and not enter him, just ride him around and let him get used to a busy show ground."

"Really?" Finny patted Sky, thrilled.

"Yeah, I think we should. Has he ever been on a trailer?" Vel asked.

Joe and Finny looked at each other.

"I doubt it," Finny said. "Can you imagine getting him this far and he won't load? What a nightmare that would be."

Nothing about training Sky had been easy. Teaching horses to load could be difficult even with a cooperative horse.

"If you kids could break this horse, I know you can get him in a trailer. Finny, let's run to the feed store to see if there are any flyers for upcoming shows," Vel said.

Finny dismounted. "Joe, would you mind taking care of Sky?"

"Not at all." Finny handed Joe the reins. "Can you believe this, Joe? Us at a horse show!" Finny gave Joe a quick, excited kiss, then ran for Vel's truck.

Vel pulled up to the feed store and kept her truck idling, knowing Finny wouldn't be long. Finny jumped out and was disappointed not to see Dale's car. He was now dating Clara from Silver Spur and Finny was happy for them both.

Sharon, the feed store manager, was working the counter.

"What can I do for you, Finny? Alfalfa is on sale."

"No feed, just looking for any show flyers."

"Really?"

"Yeah, looking for a show to take my horse to." Finny scanned the large bulletin board.

"You mean the crazy out-of-control one that sent Jeff Hastings to the hospital?"

Finny froze.

"I heard it attacks people."

"No, that's not . . . completely true . . . and he's gotten a lot better." Finny saw a flyer for the next show and grabbed it.

"It is true. I saw him run into Silver Spur and attack all the horses in the ring," a voice said from behind Finny.

Finny spun around. It was Sasha from Silver Spur, Elsa's best friend.

"Jeff said the horse is totally rogue and should be put down."

"No, he's fine and getting better every day." Finny's eyes were burning.

"Do us all a favor and let us know if you're going to a show, so we can all stay home where it's safe."

Finny turned her back on Sasha and hurried to the truck.

"Apparently Sky is famous," she told Joe as she climbed out of the truck.

"Famous, how?" he asked.

"Infamous I mean. The lady at the feed store knew who he was, practically laughed at the thought of him going to a show. Then Sasha from Silver Spur was there saying he's dangerous and Jeff thinks he should be put down."

"You're kiddin' me. What did you say?"

"Not much. I was so horrified I split."

"Did you get a flyer?"

"I did. Here." Finny handed Joe the paper.

"A week from now. I think we can get him into a trailer by then. I say let's go!"

"That's what Vel said, too, but I'm not going to think about it so I don't freak out."

Joe laughed and hugged her. "It's gonna be great, you'll see." Finny squeezed him tight.

"Did you get more joint supplement and grain? We're almost out of both," Joe said.

"Oh, no, didn't think to check. Sorry, I'm such a dope."

"Let's go now."

Finny sighed out a breath. "I don't think I could show my face there."

"We'll go to Colton County then. Prices are better anyway, it'd be worth the drive."

"Maybe there are show flyers there too, out where no one's ever heard of Sky."

"I think you'd need the next state for that," Joe said.

Finny punched him in the arm. "You're so not funny."

Forty-five minutes later, Joe, newly licensed, drove Vel's truck into the Colton Feed and Supply parking lot. It was the first time either one had been to this much larger store. Joe headed inside as Finny checked the bulletin board outside for show flyers.

Thirty seconds later Joe came bolting out the door and jumped back in the truck. He started the engine. "Finny get in!"

"Joe, what about the stuff we need? What's wrong?"

"Later, hurry!"

Finny, unnerved, jumped in and slammed the door. Joe sped out of the feed store parking lot.

"What happened?"

Joe looked out the truck's back window. "I saw someone I used to know, someone who works for my uncle."

"Oh God, did he see you?"

"I don't think so." Joe looked over his shoulder again.

"Do you think your uncle is out here?"

"He's never come this far west before. I don't know why he would now."

"What do you think that guy was doing here?"

"Don't know that either. He runs horses and cattle and other things. He's a lowlife—he'd steal from his own grandmother." Joe looked behind them again, let out a breath, and slumped back on the seat.

"I'm sorry we came all this way for nothing."

"It's no big deal." She could plainly see how distressed he was.

"Finny, is there a fairground around here?"

"I think so."

Joe nodded but stayed quiet.

"I can find out," Finny offered. "If there's a rodeo going that could explain why he's here."

Joe nodded again, still distracted by his racing thoughts. Finny grabbed her cell phone and made some calls. Two minutes later she had her answer.

"There's a rodeo there for the rest of the week. That must be why he's here."

Joe didn't answer.

"What's going on? You look totally freaked and seeing you—a person that isn't afraid of anything—scared is, well, scary."

"Sorry, Finny. Seeing him just . . . took me by surprise."

"Are you worried about your uncle?"

Joe let out a sigh and rubbed his eyes. "He's really bad news."

"What happened, Joe? You've never told me why you ran."

"I crossed the line, betrayed him. I was pretty sure he was going to kill me."

"Are you serious?" Finny grabbed his arm and held it. Joe glanced behind them again before looking over at Finny. He gave her a half smile.

"I don't know why I didn't go earlier. I was stupid."

"Don't say that. You were fifteen! Striking out on your own isn't supposed to come up for three more years. Please tell me what happened."

"I was getting older, starting to question things. Uncle John didn't like it when I asked questions. He didn't like it when I spoke, period. We didn't live normal. I know I told you we traveled in a truck and a camper. Uncle John slept in the camper and I slept in the backseat of the truck unless we were working a rodeo or a sale. Then he'd get a hotel room and sleep there. I still slept in the truck but at least got a place to shower and better food."

Finny looked over at Joe when he paused his story. He was staring straight ahead.

"I pretty much grew up with the horses in the mountains. They were my family. The babies I'd watched being born were now four years old and down with us at the sale. I'd gentled most of them and they were fit and ready for families. You know, it may seem mean to take horses out of the wild, but these days, horses don't survive to old age out there and the government needs to keep the population down so sometimes they're killed. I worked with them every day to get them ready for lives with people. What I hoped would be good lives with people." Joe went quiet again and she saw his face change. He didn't look like the self-assured person he had become; he looked like the scared kid she'd found behind the bus stop. Finny noticed that even though Joe's gaze stayed mostly on the road ahead, he still periodically checked behind them.

"So the day before the sale, six of our twenty-seven horses were in another pen. I always hung out to talk to anyone who looked at my horses so I could tell them all about them. But six were in a different section and no-body was going there. Two of the horses were so good they were kid-ready. I saw a family looking and I told them about Spirit in the next corral. The dad tells me, that corral is for the horses going to slaughter. I heard that and flipped. I ran to my uncle who was sitting by our truck and told him what happened, how there was this mistake and our horses were in the wrong corral. He looked at his buddies hanging out, drinking with him, and they all bust out laughing. He told me they were there because that's where he put 'em. They were small and plain and he'd get more money per pound for their meat than we would in the sale."

Joe went quiet for the third time. Finny bit her lip and glanced over.

"I sorta lost it. Knowing it'd do no good, I begged him to change his mind. All of them were broke and gentle. He didn't care. He hated me, Finny . . . I mean, through to the core, hated me. He'd kill the horses just because I loved them."

"Joe, my God, I'm so sorry."

"He told his drunk buddies he needed to have a man-to-man talk with me so they split. Uncle John was wasted. He was mean when he was sober and a nightmare when he was drunk. He puts his arm 'round me like he's gonna say something nice and punches me in the stomach. Then he slams me up against the truck and tells me I'm an embarrassment to him, cryin' and carryin' on. And how I'm useless and no good for anything just like my dad . . . saying how my dad betrayed him, destroyed their whole family. He slams me into the truck again and then goes off, like he's crazy. He screams at me, *It's your fault; it's your fault. She would have come back to me if it weren't for you. She loved me first.* . . . He was talking about my mother, Finny.

I think that's what drove them apart, why they hated each other. They both loved my mother. When he was telling me this . . . the look in his eyes." Joe took a deep breath. Finny squeezed his arm.

"Joe, you never have to see him again, ever."

"I know." Joe pulled into the driveway of Azure Hills and parked the truck. He turned to face Finny.

"After that he shoves me in the camper, tells me I got four hours to rest up before the race, then locks me in."

"Is that the day you ran?"

Joe nodded. "All I could think about was how to get my horses out of that pen and out of that sale. When my uncle came for me I had a plan. When the race started, I'd break off, open their gate, and get them running. Then I'd lead them out to the mountains and set them free.

"So, the race is about to begin. I'd been threatened by the other riders, and they're at it again. But somethin's different this time. They're whispering back and forth to each other, glaring at me. The bell rings. I blast off; I don't want my uncle to think I'm doing anything but trying to win. Once we round the first corner and I'm out of sight I pull out and run to the corrals. I swing open the gate, circle the herd, and they start going. They followed me right out the gate, up the road, then along the highway. It worked perfect. We ran all night, got to the base of the mountain, and they didn't need me anymore. They ran for home. It was dark but the moon was full and I could see them so clearly as they made their way up. It felt so good. I knew my uncle wouldn't find them again. He didn't know where they lived. Only I did."

"You got them free, Joe. You saved their lives."

"It was worth it, no matter what."

"Then what did you do?"

"Well, the next part of my plan I didn't think out so good." Joe let out a small laugh. "I rode the rest of the night back in the direction of the sale. I wanted to hook up with this cowboy who owned cutting horses. He'd always been real nice to me, taught me a lot about reining and told me I was a real good hand. He took good care of his animals and never sold any to slaughter. I figured I'd ask him for a job and go with him. By the time I was back it was almost dawn. I slipped the horse I'd run with back in his pen and went to where the cutting horses were, but the barn was empty. I should have known he'd be gone. He didn't participate in the illegal stuff. So there I am, nowhere to go, not a dime to my name, just the clothes on my back. I didn't know what to do. So I went up in the hay barn to hide until my uncle gave up looking for me and left.

"I was so tired, I slept the whole day. When I woke up, it was almost dark. I crawled out of the hay and looked out of the barn window. My uncle's truck was gone. I peeked out the door, didn't see a soul, so I go outside and they're on me in an instant. These cowboys from the race—it's like they were waiting for me. This is where I got my knee busted. Anyway, next thing I know it's dark and I'm looking up at my uncle. He's trying to pull me to my feet but my right leg won't work. He hauls me up and drags me to the truck, opens the camper, and shoves me in. Before he closes the door he asks me if my leg's broke. I tell him I think so. His face goes all dark and he says, 'Well, you're completely useless to me now,' and slams the door."

Finny had gone white as a sheet.

"By now I'm positive he's gonna kill me. He gets in and starts drivin'. I'd say we'd been on the road about thirty minutes and I start looking for anything to knock the hinges off the door or bust out the lock. The camper is full of junk so I'm hoping for anything. What I find is a can with three hundred dollars. That had to be a sign—for once some luck on my side. I find an old screwdriver and start prying away at the door. A few minutes later, I popped it. We were going 'bout seventy and I'm holding the door so it doesn't bang around. It took another twenty minutes; finally he stopped at a light. I was out and in the woods in ten seconds flat. And, you know the rest."

Joe closed his eyes. He felt like he'd just run a marathon. Finny scooted next to him, put her arms around his waist, and laid her head on his chest. Joe wrapped his arms around her and pulled her close. They sat in the truck and stayed in each other's arms until everything felt good again.

Chapter Twenty-Three

―――――

"I'M GOING TO BE SICK."

"No you're not. Take a deep breath and relax."

"Elsa and everyone from Silver Spur is here," Finny said, slumped on her tack trunk.

Joe knelt down so he was eye level with her. "It doesn't matter; they don't matter. We're just getting Sky in the ring to see what he can do. We're not here to win. We're here to train because that's what we do."

Finny looked up and gave Joe a smile. "You're right. I'm getting on."

"Good, just slow and relaxed, that's all we need." They led Sky over to the warm-up arena and Joe gave Finny a leg up. She entered and picked up a trot. Sky flowed soft and smooth under her, not at all bothered by the new place or all the strange horses.

"How does he feel?"

"Good. Ready."

"Super. Three ahead of you." Finny nodded and cued Sky into a canter. Out of the corner of her eye she saw Elsa and Carl watching. She had to stop caring about what they thought or did and erased them from her mind.

Sky loped easy on a huge stride. Finny collected him up for ten strides, then opened his step for ten to get him limber. Sky listened and responded perfectly.

Sky had learned to love jumping. Finny, so accurate with her ride to the jumps, gave Sky the confidence he needed. In no time they'd built a mutual bond of trust and Sky had come to listen and respond to Finny even more than to Joe.

Joe watched Finny warm up Sky. A proficient Western rodeo rider, he was new to the English world of jumpers, but he'd learned so much from Vel he felt confident enough to help Finny get through this monumental day. Joe couldn't imagine not being here with Finny and felt grateful again to Vel, who had insisted he go and she'd stay to take care of the ranch.

"Finny, you're next. Let's go watch the rider on course now." She nodded and followed Joe to the gate.

"Joe, I'm totally gonna throw up."

"No you're not. Look at the course, think about that."

"Okay, I've looked at the course. You're right, I'm not going to be sick. I'm gonna die."

Joe laughed and patted Sky. "Sky, if Finny dies make

sure you finish the course anyway."

"Again with the comedy!"

"Finny," Joe said, "you're going to be great. Go prove me right."

Finny took a deep breath and entered the ring. She waited for the whistle, then picked up a canter and rode her pace circle. She felt Sky brighten on the way to the first jump. He understood this was different from a lesson; this time it counted. Sensing that filled Finny with confidence. The goal was a double clean round. They weren't going for the win. Jump one, a simple vertical, right on stride, felt perfect. The next jump, a black and white oxer, was again easy. Sky was soft as a feather in Finny's hand. Jump after jump smooth, each turn effortless. Finny picked up a little bit of speed to the last fence, a three-foot brick wall—just like the one Sky had jumped at home dozens of times. She'd taken a bit too long getting through the course and didn't want a time fault. Sky opened his already giant stride and flew over the wall with a second to spare. The announcer called number six hundred eleven, clean first round. This meant Finny had made it to the second round—the jump-off. That's where it counted to win.

The whistle blew, telling Finny she had forty-five seconds to get to her first jump. She looked at Joe and saw him clapping away. Finny cued for the canter; this time she built a little more speed. Going for the win wasn't the plan, but Sky was going so well, she decide try for the tight turns to see how Sky handled it. As big as he was, he could still turn fast and hard when asked.

Jump one was another simple vertical, then, after a right turn, six strides to a solid green gate. Sky just stepped over, wasn't even trying. Next a combination, one stride in tight, two out long to an oxer. Sky eased through the next two. Just three jumps to go, then the gallop through the timers. Finny picked up speed, clearing the next one with a foot to spare. She collected Sky up, made the hard right, and got to jump nine at an angle. No problem for a horse with Sky's scope. In the long gallop to ten, she let Sky open up. He surged forward and closed the gap in seven strides instead of eight, then flew over the last jump. Finny kicked him forward and blasted him through the timers. It was over, she was alive, and they had made it through both rounds clean. She looked at Joe. His arms were crossed; he didn't look happy. Finny pulled on the reins and brought Sky down to the walk. She hadn't followed the plan. She went for the win the first time out on a green horse. Not the smartest thing to do, even if it did work out. The announcer called out, "Clean round, twenty-one point six. Our current leader." That was exciting to hear. It didn't mean someone wouldn't come along and beat their time, but it was a very nice first time out. Joe's unhappy expression hadn't changed by the time she rode up to him.

"Finny, I know it worked out, but you know how he is. When you angled jump nine he could have hit it, or worse crashed through it. Then he would think shows are scary. You know how sensitive he is. You know what it took to get him here."

"Joe, you're right. I'm sorry. He just felt like a million bucks. He didn't look at a thing. He was featherlight the whole time. It just felt right."

Joe rubbed his temples. "It was his first time out, and he's way harder than most horses."

Finny realized he was mad at her for being childish. For Joe, who was never allowed to be a child, this was unforgivable.

"Joe, I totally see that now. I could have undone everything you accomplished with him. I'm sorry, really."

Joe sat down on a bench just outside the warm-up ring. "You know what, Finny? I'm sorry. It's your horse, your first show. You have every right to have fun. I think I'm turning into my uncle yelling at you like that, minus the cursing." Joe put his face in his hands.

Finny hopped off of Sky and sat next to him. "This is our business and I intend to treat it like that from now on. If we make a plan, I'll stick to it." Finny laced her fingers through his.

"You know, Finny, you looked pretty amazing out there. And Sky, he steps over those jumps, like he's not even tryin.'"

"That's what it feels like, Joe."

"What are the times? Anyone beat us yet?"

Finny got up and checked the board. "No, two others have gone, five more to go. We're still leading." Joe stood and looked at the board.

"Wow . . . Is there prize money for this class?"

"Five hundred bucks."

"Oh man, I hope you win."

"You mean *we* win! Do you realize if we win that money, we can start getting some training equipment?"

"That last horse was two seconds slower. If we get that money, let's buy a bitting rig and some bridles. We might just be able to pull off this training business."

Finny grabbed Joe's hand. "You know we will." Sky nudged her shoulder, as if to say, *Hey, don't forget about the star here.* Finny rubbed his neck, but kept her eyes on the ring.

Hand in hand, Joe and Finny watched the last horse go. He finished the ride a tenth of a second short. Sky had won. Joe and Finny's delighted cheers were cut short by another announcement. There was a last-minute entry.

"I don't believe it; it's Elsa," Finny said, feeling ill.

"Doesn't she normally show at three-six level or higher? What's she doing in the training class?"

"Yeah, she's probably never done a training class in her life. She buys all her horses made."

"Is she even allowed to do this class?"

"It's an open class. Anyone can do it."

"She's doing this just to make sure you don't win, isn't she?"

"That would be my guess."

Joe put his arm around Finny and held her tight. They watched Elsa enter the ring on a horse that cost more than most houses. Savannah, her chestnut mare, was fit and sleek and used to doing jumps much higher. The whistle blew and Elsa kicked her horse forward. She finished the first round with ease as well as the fastest first-round time. The whistle blew for the jump-off. Elsa dashed off.

"I don't think I can stand to watch. There goes our bitting rig."

"It's okay, Finny. We'll get one next time."

Elsa was flying around the jumps as fast as she could, almost frantic.

"She's going too fast," Finny said.

"Isn't that the point?"

"Not if you want to win. Going that fast, you can't turn—she's being reckless."

Joe and Finny watched Elsa tear up the course. Turning wide, kicking like crazy. As she cleared the second-to-last fence, her time was close to Sky's.

"Joe, she's going to try to leave out a stride like Sky

did, but Savannah doesn't have Sky's stride." Finny put her hand to her mouth as Elsa whipped her horse to the last jump. Savannah, in a panic, leaped forward and tried to jump when her rider asked. She couldn't make it; her legs swam. The mare crashed into the last jump and somersaulted in the air, tearing the hard lumber of the jump to pieces before hitting the ground in a bone-crushing crash. The whole crowd gasped collectively, then fell silent.

"Oh my God." Finny buried her face into Joe's chest. Within seconds Jeff and Barbara and others from Silver Spur were running into the arena. Neither Elsa, who had been flung free, nor her horse was moving. The crowd of spectators ran to the edge of the ring, obscuring the view from Joe and Finny.

"Joe, tell me she's okay."

Joe hugged her. "I can't tell. I can't see anything." The paramedics and ambulance rolled in with no sirens, so as not to spook the horses. Joe and Finny moved down the rail, leading Sky, to see if they could spot Elsa. Some of the crowd had dispersed but the EMTs were now surrounding her, blocking the view. A small group of bystanders and a veterinarian were hovering over Savannah, who still hadn't moved. Joe watched the vet stand up after checking the mare and wrap his stethoscope around his neck. Joe knew by the vet's body language that the horse was dead.

Finny began to cry. When Joe looked at her she was staring at Savannah. She knew it, too. The EMTs lifted the stretcher holding Elsa into the ambulance. Finny saw the oxygen mask on her face. That told her what she needed to know. It was a relief to know she was alive.

"Let's get out of here," whispered Joe. Finny nodded and once the ambulance doors closed, they made their way to the barn with Sky by their side. Neither one spoke as they untacked and got Sky ready for the trip home. Joe hurried to the parking lot to get his truck, which they'd hitched to Vel's trailer.

As they had feared the week before, Sky had been impossible to load. After several days and endless hours, Joe, who used every trick in the book, was out of ideas. He couldn't get Sky near the trailer, much less in it. Joe, too tired to keep trying, unclipped the lead from Sky's halter to let him graze on his own. He sat on the bumper trying to figure out how to break the news to Finny, when Sky came up wanting the carrots in his hand. Out of frustration, Joe tossed them into the trailer and told Sky to go fetch. Without hesitation Sky walked into the trailer after the carrots. Joe didn't know whether to laugh or cry. As long as it was Sky's idea, he was happy to do it.

Using the same technique today, they loaded Sky in and latched the gate.

The Silver Spur trailer drove past them, then pulled out of the show grounds.

"Finny, Elsa killed her horse and almost herself, just to try to beat you," Joe marveled.

"From the day I set foot on that ranch, she's hated me and I don't know why."

"We need to break all ties with her. We'll go to the next county to show if we have to. She worries me; she's not right."

"You think she might be dangerous? Like she might try to hurt Sky or something?"

"After today, I think she's capable of anything."

Chapter Twenty-Four

———

"THANKS AGAIN FOR THE RIDE, DALE. I SURE APpreciate it."

"No problem. See ya tomorrow." Dale gave Finny a smile, then backed his car out of the Azure Hills drive.

Finny jogged up the drive and found Joe in the round pen, lunging Jenna, the four-year-old quarter horse mare they had in training. Finny smiled when she saw the new bitting rig on the horse. It kept Jenna's body framed correctly while she worked free of a rider.

"She looks great!"

"She is. She's so easy, I think she was born broke."

"Dale filled me in on Elsa. She had a bad concussion, but she's okay and already out of the hospital."

"That's good to hear," Joe said with a mystified shake of his head.

"Any work to be finished before Sky?"

"No, got it done."

"You should save something for me, you know."

Joe smiled, "Sorry, I gotta keep myself busy while you're gone. It's lonely here without you."

"You could go to high school like everyone else."

Joe shook visibly; his eyes got big. "I've seen your high school—terrifying!"

Finny had to laugh. "Can't argue there."

Joe eased the mare to a walk and allowed her to cool down. Vel came out of the house with several slips of paper in her hand.

"Uh, kids?" She was scratching her head. "I just checked the message machine, and, well, these are for you."

Finny took the messages, then covered her mouth with her hand. "Joe, these people want their horses trained, with you . . . and me! Look, this one wants her horse taught to jump, these two need young horses broke, and this one needs some corrective training. Joe, that's five horses in training, at six hundred dollars apiece. That's three thousand dollars a month. Joe, three thousand a month!"

Joe, suddenly dizzy, used the fence to steady himself.

With a huge smile, Vel said, "Apparently the word about Sky got around. Winning that class did more than prove to yourselves what you can do. It showed the community what you two are capable of. You both should be very proud." Vel gave them both hugs and went back into her house.

"Joe, five horses in training. Do you know what that means?"

Joe nodded his head, his mind far away.

"What about putting an ad out, or a sign on the road. Maybe we can get some students going also. How cool would that be!"

"It would be great. I don't know about a sign on the road though."

"I can see it now, McCoy Training Center. I'm calling these people right now!"

Joe, still in shock, watched Finny run to the house. The news was so good. He wanted to be happy and get his name out there in the horse world, be legit and do it for real. Knowing his uncle was out there somewhere, looking for him, made that impossible.

Twenty minutes later Finny was back. "Joe, two horses are coming tomorrow, the other two at the end of the month. In a couple of weeks you'll have three thousand dollars in your hand."

"*We* will. You're my business partner, don't forget."

"Right. This is amazing, Joe, amazing! Once school is out, I'll be able to do more. Maybe we could take on more horses."

"I know we could. My parents ran a string of fifteen."

"Wow, can you imagine!" Finny, giddy, was jumping up and down.

Joe gave a restrained nod.

"You okay?" Finny went somber seeing his face.

"Yeah. Just can't believe this is happening."

"Good things happening, is a good thing—remember that."

Joe smiled and nodded.

Finny kissed him firm on the mouth. "I'm going to get Sky."

Finny took her time grooming Sky before she tacked him up. Often, when she had a ton of homework, she hurried, keeping her rides short so she could get home in time to get it done. Her mom had made it clear that she could keep horsing around only as long as she kept her grades up. But lately her mom had been complaining that they never saw her anymore. Finny couldn't believe it. When she wanted attention she couldn't get anyone to notice her. Now that she wanted to spend all her time with Joe and Sky, suddenly she was missed.

At least this was Friday and Monday was a holiday—the whole long weekend stretched before her.

Once in the arena she allowed Sky to warm up. Joe

was by the rail a minute later, wanting to discuss an idea he had.

"What about using some of the money to buy an investment horse? We could get one from the sale for a few hundred and turn it around for a few thousand once it's broke. That's what my mom and dad used to do."

"Sounds like a great idea. How much do we need?"

"About five hundred."

"Let's do it." A flash of light caught Finny's eye. She looked toward Silver Spur. "Joe, do you see something just up the hill behind Silver Spur's fence line?"

Joe stood on the fence to get a better view. "No."

"There it is again. A flash of light—did you see it?"

"Yeah, that's weird. Who would be up there?" Joe strained to see as far as he could.

"It's two people on horses. They're turning away." Finny watched as the riders disappeared into the brush.

"I do see. They had to come from Silver Spur to get back there."

"You think it was a camera flash?" Finny asked.

"No. Definitely not. I think it was a reflection from binoculars. Finny . . . I think we're being watched."

Sleep, when it came, was fitful and didn't last. Joe gazed at the stars through the window and then closed his eyes and named off the constellations. He opened them again and looked at the clock on his nightstand. Five o'clock. Joe rubbed his face and pushed the covers back and got out of bed. He thanked the heavens for making everything so good for him. Unfortunately it was because everything was so good that he was getting nervous. Typically good times didn't last and Joe felt his luck was going to turn.

It was the people in the hills that had him on edge. Finny thought it was Elsa, keeping and eye on them, but Joe didn't think so. The two riders were in Western saddles, not English. Joe knew from his brief stint at Silver Spur that no one there owned a Western saddle. It was possible the riders had nothing to do with Silver Spur.

As quietly as he could, Joe got dressed and went outside. It was late fall and the pre-dawn air was chilly. Not wanting to bother to go back inside for a jacket, Joe dealt with the cold by rubbing his arms. He circumnavigated the property, peeking into stalls, finding most of the horses asleep. Even if that man from the feed store last week did see him, Joe reasoned, he wouldn't know to go all the way to the next county to find him at a small, obscure horse rescue.

Joe realized Sky's winning performance at the show got him noticed. Other people now knew how to get in touch with him. Could the news somehow have gotten back to his uncle? Joe considered he might be overthinking his importance to the man. But he knew his uncle was vindictive and vengeful. It wasn't just the race and the money lost. Joe was the daily in-the-flesh reminder of his ultimate betrayal, the reason he had lost the woman he loved.

The more Joe thought about it, the more things in his past became clear. He'd wondered why his uncle, who clearly didn't like or want him, took him, instead of another relative or even foster care. When he was too young to understand, his uncle had told him his parents weren't just rolling but spinning in their graves because he took him in. Joe remembered his uncle laughing when he said it. At the time he thought that was a good thing, meaning they were happy, because his uncle was happy. Joe later came to find out it meant the opposite.

Walking toward Sky's corral, Joe rubbed his arms again to warm them. He looked into the pen. It was empty. It's front gate was closed and latched. Knowing Sky couldn't jump out because they had made his gates so high, he checked the back gate. It was open. The stars were bright and the moon was full. Joe could see fresh hoofprints from a walking horse in the soil softened by the night's dew. He followed them to the back of the property and out the gate. Joe looked at the chain that kept the gate locked. Someone had used bolt cutters.

Joe scanned the area as far as he could but knew it was too late. Sky was gone.

Joe held his arms around a sobbing Finny and tried not to cry himself. Vel was beside herself, pacing back and forth. Horse thieves were a thing of the past. She didn't know what to do.

"We'll call the police."

"Vel, don't," Joe said. "It will only make things worse."

"Joe, you don't even have to be around when they come."

Joe stroked Finny's hair, doing his best to comfort her.

"If what I think happened, did happen, police getting involved would only make it worse."

Finny lifted her head, her eyes beet red. "How would it make it worse?"

"If the people who I think have him knew police were snooping around they'd panic . . ."

". . . And kill him." Finny finished the sentence for Joe.

"I think so."

Finny sagged in his arms. Joe held her and kissed her forehead.

"Who do you think has him?" Vel asked.

"Ray and his buddies. I know he used to cowboy and he would know how to get rid of Sky fast. I have a feeling he's doing this for Jeff."

"What makes you think that, Joe?"

"First thing Jeff told me when I started working there was to keep Elsa happy at all cost. Her daddy bankrolls Silver Spur and when Elsa ain't happy, no one's happy."

Vel continued to pace, "Much as I hate to think he would, you kids beating him on a horse he couldn't handle and deemed rogue would hurt his reputation pretty bad." Vel rubbed her forehead as her pacing got faster. "I've known Jeff for twenty years. He'd do anything to keep his reputation and his big payday client intact."

"Vel, Sky won't get into a trailer the normal way. There's no way they'll be able to load him, especially if they get tough with him. Once Sky gets mad he'll be impossible to control. They'll have to ride or herd him out of the area."

"Then what should we do?" Finny said between sobs.

"I gotta go to Silver Spur, see if I can find out anything."

"What about Carl and Ray?"

"That's who I'm going to talk to."

"Joe, don't. What if they get mad?" Finny said.

"I intend to make them mad."

"Joe," Vel said, "I don't think this is a good idea. I

can't let you get hurt." She crossed her arms. As much confidence as she had in Joe, he was still a kid and she was the adult.

Joe was growing frustrated and time was running out. It was already 6 AM. Joe's guess was that Sky had been taken around 2 AM. The longer they waited, the farther Sky and whoever had him would get. "Go with me then, but stay in the truck. I need to talk to them alone."

"Fine. Let's go."

They all piled into Vel's truck and headed to Silver Spur. The sun hadn't yet crested the horizon but pre-dawn light filled the sky. As they turned into the gates Vel's apprehension grew. Vel parked behind the barn just as Carl turned the corner. Joe jumped out before anyone could stop him.

"Carl!" Joe yelled. That stopped the man in his tracks.

"What are you doing here?" Joe noticed Carl walked with a slight limp. He was sure it was thanks to Sky.

"You took Sky, didn't you?"

Carl's gaze didn't waver.

"Sky hurt your foot, didn't he?"

Carl's eyes got big before they narrowed.

"Get off this property," Carl hissed.

"You don't remember the first time we met, do you?"

"What are you talking about? You heard me, get!"

"It was right here—skinny, sick kid with a broken leg, you beat me up pretty good, stole my money, remember? Well, I'm not sick or skinny now, and my leg's fine." Joe followed his statement with a smashing right to Carl's face. The punch spun Carl around and almost to the ground. Carl sputtered, looked confused, and made a feeble attempt to hit back. Joe's next punch did take him down.

Joe jogged back to the truck and hopped in. "Boy, that felt good."

"Okay, Rambo, did you find out anything?" Vel asked, trying not to sound pleased. Finny, stunned, didn't utter a word.

"I know they did it. I could see it in his face."

Vel quickly pulled out of Silver Spur and turned to Joe. "What do we do now?"

"Vel, where's the nearest horse auction?"

"Far end of Colton County. Why?"

"Jumping horses can be worth a lot of money right?"

"Yes," Vel answered.

Finny, looking wary, did her best to stop crying.

"And Sky, do you think as well as he jumps they could get twenty or thirty grand for him?"

"It's possible."

"Twenty to thirty grand is a year's worth of work for

selling one horse. Even if they were supposed to get rid of him, I bet anything they'd try to sell him. All they'd need to do was get him out of the area and far enough away where no one knows him.

"And let's say they couldn't load him," Joe went on. "They'd start to panic because everyone at Silver Spur knows who Sky is. They got to get him gone, so I'm thinking they had to ride him out. If it were me, that's what I'd do. I bet he'd take him to an auction where there'd be hundreds of horses, an easy place to hide him until he could get help to get Sky shipped out of there and far enough away to get sold."

"Are you sure about this?" Vel asked, starting to feel they were getting in over their heads.

"He won't load. Riding or leading him would be the only way to get him outta here. Please, Vel, we got to get there as fast as possible."

"What about that man from the feed store, Joe, what if he sees you?" Finny, overwhelmed, finally spoke up. As much as she loved Sky, she didn't want to risk Joe's safety.

"We'll worry about that later. Come on, we gotta go!" Vel swung the truck around and hit the gas, saying a prayer, hoping she wasn't being stupid. Her instincts were to call the police, but this was Joe's world and she trusted him.

Finny began to think more clearly. Her initial shock was turning into anger. "Joe, I'll go look through the pens. You stay out of sight. If I see him I'll grab him and go."

"No, Finny, if we find him, that's when we call the police."

"Joe, I agree with you there," Vel added.

"How much longer till we get there?" Joe asked, looking at his watch.

"About two hours. Do you think we'll be too late?"

"No, not if he won't get in a trailer, and I doubt he will. They'd have to take him out after dark."

"Why would they do this to me? I just don't understand. He's just a horse. They have a barn full of great horses." Finny tried not to cry again but the tears came back.

"Finny, honey," Vel's words were as kind as she could make them, "some people are just . . . not right, they can't take not having things go their way."

"Some people are just plain evil, like my uncle. That's why they can't take it. Not getting what they want drives them crazy. You saw what Elsa did to her own horse." Joe shut his eyes and pressed the heels of his hands to his temples in an effort stave off an oncoming headache. He had thought that once he was away from his uncle, he would be away from evil but it had come to find him, even here. He felt Finny's hand on his shoulder. Upset as she was, she was trying to comfort him. Joe put his hand over hers and instantly felt better.

"These flood control channels that are everywhere," Joe asked, looking out the truck window, "how often do they have water in them?"

"Just when it rains."

"So never this time of year?"

"No, it only rains here in the winter."

Joe contemplated the information and studied the channels as they drove.

"You think they used the channels to move Sky?" Vel asked.

"It would be the perfect way to go through a town, no obstruction for miles, easy to ride through."

"Vel, how long to the auction site?" Finny was getting anxious.

"About forty-five minutes, Finny. I know that seems forever."

"Joe, could they have come this far that fast?"

"If they used the channels, they could easy."

Vel, who normally obeyed the speed limits, pushed it to get there as quickly as possible. The road trip no one wanted kept their spirits low and talking to a minimum for most of the ride.

"There it is!" Finny yelled when she spotted the

giant "Livestock Auction Today" sign straight ahead. The place was massive. Multiple corrals and barns were lined up in row after row spanning at least fifty acres. Cattle, pigs, horses, and sheep were everywhere as far as the eye could see and the place was packed. It was all Vel could do to maneuver her pickup into the parking lot. Trucks and trailers haphazardly littered the place, from two-horse straight loads to giant two-floor stock trailers. The auction was about to begin and hundreds of people were moving horses, cattle, sheep, and hogs toward the auction pens.

"How will we ever find him here? There must be a million horses at least!" Finny said, her voice trembling. Joe grabbed a flyer that was stapled to a telephone pole. He let out a sigh, crumpled the flyer, and tossed it in a trash can. "Twenty-five hundred."

"Kids, this auction is for Western horses. Sky will be a giant in comparison. Do you all have your phones? Let's go and look, ask if anyone has seen a really big horse."

"Wait, Joe . . . what if someone here recognizes you?"

"Finny, my uncle won't come this far."

Finny heaved out a sigh and set off. "I'll go this way."

"I'm heading for the pens," Joe said.

"I'll go this way. Let's call each other in an hour regardless," Vel instructed.

Joe kept his hat low on his head. It was true, he and his uncle had never gone this far west, but it didn't mean men who knew him didn't. Joe searched the crowd for a familiar face. Someone he could trust to give him information and not give him up. Joe pressed through the throng of people on the way to the horse pens. Once there, the crowd had thinned and he spotted professional wranglers unloading horses out of a large stock trailer.

Joe stared at the men, his pulse quickening. He didn't recognize them but it was a small horse world. It frustrated him that fear was creeping into his brain. He reasoned he wasn't the skinny helpless kid he had been five months ago, and made his way to the men. Wary of outsiders, they were slow to open up, but after a few minutes found Joe was one of their own. They told him they had seen a cowboy on a little quarter horse, who had headed out earlier ponying another horse. He stuck out because he was the only one not leaving in a trailer and the horse being led was huge. Joe's pulse raced. They were on Sky's trail. He asked the wranglers if they knew who the cowboy was or where he was going. They didn't, but they directed Joe to someone who might.

Joe ran into the sales barn and asked for Raul, who was called over by one of the handlers for the auction. Joe took a chance and told him that he was looking for a giant bay that had been stolen and most likely wouldn't load into a trailer. Raul called a couple more cowboys over for help. Joe studied their faces. He didn't recognize them but was getting uncomfortable. His race wins had made him well known. He didn't have to recognize someone for a man to know who he or his uncle was. One of the cowboys said he'd be right back, looked at Joe one more time, then walked away. Joe noticed that the man pulled his cell out of his pocket before rounding the corner. He realized he needed to speed things up, to get out of there as fast as he could. "Any idea where there's an auction like this that sells both English and Western horses?"

"Stockton's the only one I know. That's a few hours north of here."

The cowboy who had used the phone came back.

"I know where your man's going." Joe saw the cowboy's companion raise his eyebrows in surprise and glance at his friend.

"Where?"

"Campground two hours ride east of here. Horses can be housed overnight."

"Campground? What's the name?"

"Sun Valley."

Joe knew the man was lying. He could see it in his body language and in how intently he was now staring at him. It made no sense to go east. The cowboy would go north to get to Stockton. Joe felt sick. The man in front of him was setting him up. Joe wondered what price his uncle had put on his head.

"Thanks for your help."

"We're heading that way, we'll give you a lift."

Joe backed away as he spoke. "No, got a car, thanks." Confident they weren't going to try to stop him, Joe turned and hurried back toward the truck. He called Finny and Vel and told them what he found out about Sky and nothing else; no need to worry them more.

Joe knew he had to catch up to the cowboy who had taken Sky before he got to his next destination. In the distance a train whistle blew. The revelation hit. The tracks followed the flood control channels. That was how he was going to catch up. The more he thought about it, the more he was convinced it was the only way. He also knew he had to do this alone. It was too dangerous for Finny, who had parents to go home to, and if he told Vel his plan, she would do whatever it took to stop him. Joe spotted Finny and Vel at the truck. His mind raced. They'd stop him. Joe knew this was the only chance to get Sky back. He turned and ran toward the sound of the train. It was loud, so he knew it couldn't be far. His phone rang. It was Finny. He kept going and ignored the phone. He spotted the tracks, ran to them, and followed them north. His phone rang again. He picked it up.

"Joe, where are you?"

"Finny, I think I know how to find Sky. Tell Vel to take you home so you don't get in trouble. I got my phone and plenty of money on me. I'll call you the second I know something. I love you. I'm sorry." Joe hung up, held the phone to his head, and said a prayer. It rang immediately, only to be drowned out by the sound of an oncoming train. Joe looked behind him; a cargo train was slowly approaching. Jumping on was a breeze and Joe was on his way.

Finny hung up the phone for the third time. She clutched it to her chest and closed her eyes. She told Vel that Joe had found an old friend of his and this cowboy knew where Sky was. "He's going with him and will call us as soon as he knows something." Finny tried not to shake visibly and couldn't look at Vel having so blatantly lied to her.

"Joe took off, just like that?" Vel's brows furrowed, confused.

"This is the world he was raised in. I guess he knows what he's doing."

"Call him again, Finny. I'm not comfortable leaving

here without him."

"He knew we wouldn't let him go. That's why he took off. He's not answering his phone."

"Let me try." Vel dialed and the phone went straight to voice mail. "Finny, let's get in the truck and drive around and look for him."

"Okay, but it won't do any good. He's gone."

Vel dropped Finny off at home, then continued on to Azure Hills. Finny dashed into her house and asked her mom if she could stay at Azure Hills the rest of the weekend because Vel wasn't feeling well and really needed her help. Finny swore she'd spend the next weekend with her sisters to make up for it. Beth reluctantly agreed. Finny hugged her mom, then ran to her room and shoved money, clothes, and supplies into her backpack. Last, she scoured the garage and found a detailed map that showed the flood channels as well as the railroad tracks. She had heard a train whistle blow in the background when she had been on the phone with Joe. Finny knew him well enough to figure out what he was doing. Next she checked online and looked up the dates and locations of every rodeo or sale she could find north of them. The closest one that was near the railroad tracks was Stockton.

Before she set off, she sent Joe a text: *I love you; please tell me you're safe and where you are so I don't go crazy.* Finny jumped on her bike and rode hard for the ranch. Pumped on adrenaline, she got there in no time. Finny hid her bike behind the barn, grabbed her saddle and bridle, went to Joe's truck, and got behind the wheel. She looked in the glove box and found the key. The old Ford roared to life. She figured Joe might regret having taught her to drive but she doubted that. He wasn't in this alone. Finny pulled out, hoping Vel wouldn't figure out what she'd done when she noticed Joe's truck was gone.

Joe scanned the culverts as the train slowly rumbled by. Night was falling. Most likely the cowboy would be going slowly to conserve the horses' strength, so Joe reasoned it was possible for the train to catch up. He prayed it would before they hit the next town. Joe knew once the cowboys discovered he hadn't fallen for their trick and gone to Sun Valley, they'd figure out where he had gone.

Guilt hung around his neck like a noose. Joe glanced at his phone. He powered it back on and found Finny's message. Her words cut through him. Maybe he was out of his mind doing what he'd done, waltzing back into his uncle's world knowing he was looking for him. Joe groaned out loud with uncertainty. He was being foolish doing this alone. He was glad he was out there looking, but keeping Finny in the dark wasn't fair. They were a team . . . well, more than a team. They were each other's family. Joe checked the time. It was after 1 AM. He leaned back against the open door of the train and watched the culvert. He texted Finny back.

I'm on a train heading north following the culverts. No luck so far. I love you and I'm sorry.

Joe shut his phone and scanned the dark. He wished clouds weren't covering the moon so he could see better.

The train rolled steadily down the track. The rhythmic rocking of the rail car was trying to put him to sleep. Joe rubbed his eyes and got up and stretched, doing his best to rouse himself. He'd been on the train too long. Maybe he was wrong about what the cowboy had done; maybe Sky *had* been taken to Sun Valley. Joe worried his paranoia had clouded his judgment.

He would have kept torturing himself with doubt had he not spotted a rider ponying a giant horse in the culvert below him. Joe stepped back away from the door as they passed. He wanted to be well ahead of them when he got off. Joe sat on the floor with his feet dangling off the side. The train wasn't moving very fast, but it was fast enough when Joe jumped, tucked, and rolled. The gravel tore at his shirt and his skin, drawing a little blood from his shoulder, but he survived and got quickly to his feet. Joe hid in the bushes until the rider passed. Joe knew the man would soon stop; they'd been going all day. He was relieved to be right again. Two miles later the cowboy rode up out of the culvert and onto a trail. Just up ahead were corrals.

Making his way as quietly as he could, Joe got as close as possible without being spotted. He watched the cowboy lead Sky into the corral and then untack his saddle horse and put it in with Sky. Joe scanned the area, wishing he knew where he was. The cowboy, instead of looking for a place to bunk down, got on his cell phone. Joe was close enough to recognize the man's face when his phone illuminated it. He didn't know his name, but was sure he'd seen him before. Making a call instead of bunking down for the night was a bad sign. He wanted the man to fall asleep so he could take Sky and run, but now he'd have to wait and see.

Joe sized the man up. The cowboy lifestyle kept a body tough and the man in front of him was no push-over. The cowboy checked his phone again and then leaned against the fence before shoving his hands in his pockets. Joe wanted to punch the ground in frustration. The man was waiting for someone. Which meant more people were coming. Joe looked at his phone but couldn't risk turning it on. It made noise and if there were messages it would make even more. Joe slipped his phone back in his pocket and watched and waited.

Twenty minutes later the sound of a pickup truck coming was unmistakable. Two men climbed out once it parked. Joe's pulse raced. Why three men for two horses, and no horse trailer? It made no sense. The temptation to crawl closer to hear what was going on was strong, but prudence won out and Joe stayed where he was. He racked his brain trying to figure out why they were there. The scenario building in his head was the only thing that answered all the questions. They were there to find him. Joe's stomach twisted with nausea when he realized the cowboy from the livestock auction had recognized him, then called his uncle. Joe knew his Uncle John was in with enough seedy people to find out who had stolen Sky and he was sure a deal had been struck. Instead of going to be sold, Sky was now being used as bait.

Chapter Twenty-Five

———

"TURN YOUR PHONE ON, JOE, COME ON!" FINNY said out loud after her fifteenth unsuccessful call. She had been thrilled to get his text, but she needed to talk to him. She threw the phone to the seat in frustration. After driving most of the night she was almost to Stockton. Past getting there, she had no plan.

Dead tired from the long drive and late hour, Finny was sure it was fear, worry, and adrenaline keeping her awake. She'd never driven on major roads before and never at night and was relieved there wasn't much traffic. Seeing the road signs and watching out for police cars wasn't easy. Finny just glimpsed the "Welcome to Stockton" sign as she sped past it. She grabbed her phone and hit redial. As expected, voice mail. Now in town, Finny got off the main road when she saw a sign indicating a railroad crossing. She pulled off the lit highway onto a dark dirt road and drove slowly down it until she came to train tracks. Once there, she pulled off to the side, shut off the engine, then locked her doors. She grabbed the pillows and blankets she'd brought with her and lay down out of sight. She texted Joe, told him where she was, and got comfortable. If she didn't hear from him by morning, she was calling the police whether he liked it or not.

Something was happening. The men started to move through the brush. One man went toward the culvert, the other toward the west. The third man jumped in the back of the truck. The cover was sparse; only the black night and Joe's stillness kept him invisible. Joe stayed low and kept his eye on the man who walked within thirty feet of him. The second man passed within sixty. They were slowly moving back in the direction from which the horses had come. Joe watched the men until they were swallowed up by the dark. One of the men whistled, and a moment later an intensely bright light lit up the night. To his shock, Joe saw that the pickup had hunting lights along the roof. The man on top was slowly turning the light, searching the area. Joe, knowing he only had seconds, scrambled to his feet and ran toward the corrals. There would be nowhere to hide if the light hit him. He was making noise, too much noise. Joe slowed down but it was too late. "I hear something," rang out through the dark. "Over here." Joe dashed toward the corral and Sky. If he opened the gate and set the horses free, maybe that would distract the cowboys. If he could get on Sky fast enough, he would. The light blinded Joe when the beam hit him. He cut left to get out of it but it followed him. Not able to see, he ran blindly. Joe heard someone to his left, so he cut right and hit a wall, or what he thought was a wall until the wall grabbed him and spun him to the ground.

"Got him," the wall yelled. Joe could barely breathe; the man was kneeling on his back while twisting his arm behind him. He heard the other two men run up.

"Is it him?" a voice from the dark asked.

"Don't know." Joe felt someone grab a fistful of his hair then yank his head up. A flashlight blinded him again.

"It sure is."

Chapter Twenty-Six

FINNY WOKE TO THE TRAIN'S WHISTLE. SHE KICKED off her blankets and leapt out of the truck only to recoil from the bitter cold. She resisted the cold and watched the oncoming train. It was a cargo train . . . Joe had said he was on a cargo train. Finny's heart raced as each car rolled past her one by one. There were several empty and open cars where someone could easily jump on. Finny scanned each one. All empty. She quickly jumped back in the truck and pulled the blanket around her. Her hands were shaking when she flipped up her phone. Finny's heart sank to her feet. No messages. Knowing what she'd hear, she dialed Joe's number anyway. Voice mail.

Finny slid to the driver's seat and started the truck. She pulled out and drove down the frontage road looking for a gas station. Two miles later she found one, pulled up to a pump, and parked. After getting the gas pumping, she went to the mini mart and grabbed several granola bars, enough for Joe too, and a carton of milk. Early as it was the place was deserted except for the cashier. Finny was making her way back to the truck when another pickup pulled in. Out came what looked to Finny like a real live cowboy.

She went up to the man, feeling completely out of her element. "Excuse me, are there any rodeos or livestock auctions around here?"

"You lookin' to buy a horse, miss? If ya are I got some for sale."

"No, I'm looking for a friend who travels with the rodeo and I think he's in the area."

"Well, up the road about five miles is one set for this weekend." Finny thanked him and hurried back to her truck. She hoped against hope she'd find Joe and Sky soon. As desperately as she wanted Sky, she'd feel a thousand times better once she found Joe.

Finny couldn't stop shaking. She turned on the heat, but her trembling was from fear not cold. She'd never broken the law, left home, or lied this big to her mother. Much less driven hundreds of miles away by herself with no driver's license. She wished she was brave like Joe. He could hop on a train or gallop up a mountain. Finny's stomach twisted. Taking the truck and going after him was as close as she'd ever come to doing something brave, or totally stupid.

She ignored her first plan, which had been to call the police first thing. She now realized they would send her home, most likely without answers, after they figured out she was too young to drive. Maybe they'd even arrest her. But once at the rodeo with no call or any sign of Joe, Finny would call the police even if it would do her in.

She pictured her parents finding out: She'd be grounded for life, banned from stepping on Azure Hills property, and not allowed to see Joe ever again, and that's if they didn't kill her. Trying to hold terror at bay, Finny glanced at the phone and willed it to ring. *Why isn't he calling?* cycled through her head like a mantra. Her mind raced through a million possible reasons, all of them bad.

Chapter Twenty-Seven

PANIC EASED INTO A STEADY MISERY. JOE FInally stopped replaying in his head what he should've done because it tortured him. He thought of Finny and worried endlessly. Where was she and was she okay? He knew his uncle was capable of anything and vowed not to let him find out about her.

Out of frustration, Joe pulled on the ropes that kept his wrists firmly bound behind his back but didn't bother with the ones around his ankles. He'd given up trying to free himself hours ago because all it did was cramp his muscles and burn his skin.

Joe leaned his head back against the wall of the camper and closed his eyes. It was getting hot. The sun had been up a while and the temperature was steadily rising in the small, cramped camper. Joe figured maybe this was how his uncle would do him in. Leave him to cook as the sun turned the camper into an oven. When a bead of sweat ran down the side of his face, Joe opened his eyes and checked the camper's two small windows. Both were closed. Joe let out a shaky breath and willed his nerves to settle.

"Welcome home," his uncle had said when he saw him. That was it, *welcome home,* then camper time. Joe replayed his unemotional homecoming. It was more terrorizing than screamed curses or a beating, like a subliminal way of saying you're gonna get what's coming soon and it's gonna be bad.

A wave of relief washed over him when the door opened. Joe was grateful he wasn't crying, didn't want to give his uncle the satisfaction. The cowboy at the door grabbed the rope around his ankles and hauled him out of the camper with one pull. The blast of cool outside air was dizzying. The cowboy freed Joe, who rubbed his wrists and stared defiantly at his uncle.

Uncle John chuckled at his nephew, then shook his head. He spoke to the men by his side, "I don't think he likes me very much." The man to Joe's left let out an amused snort.

"Why is the big horse so important to you, Joe?" His uncle's tone was calm and steady. Joe noticed that his hands, now free, were shaking. He shoved them in his pockets, ignoring his uncle's question.

"You've grown. What you weigh now, one fifty, one

sixty?" Joe scanned the area past the men. He looked at his uncle for a moment. Just north of forty, he stood over six feet tall and weighed more than two hundred pounds. He was a big man, but for the first time he looked like a man to Joe, not some impossible obstacle he couldn't overcome.

"It doesn't matter, wouldn't trust you out there racing anyway." Joe stayed quiet and kept his eyes averted. Uncle John adjusted his hat and rocked back on his heels.

"I'm gonna ask you again. Why is the big horse important to you?" Joe took a deep breath and readied himself. He knew his uncle wouldn't tolerate him not answering and Joe had no intention of talking. He heard the sharp intake of breath from his uncle. Joe clamped his eyes shut. When the blow he expected didn't come he looked up.

Uncle John had pulled out a wad of bills from his pocket and handed some to the cowboy on his left. "Go buy him something to eat, but keep an eye on him since he tends to wander off. I'm gonna find out what's so special about that horse."

Finny drove into the rodeo grounds. The cold that had shocked her in the morning had been replaced by a gentle, warm breeze.

She locked the truck and scanned the grounds. There were hundreds of people and even more horses. When a quick check of her phone revealed nothing, Finny headed into the crowd. Once at the horse and cattle pens she slowly circled around them. There was action everywhere. Large livestock trucks unloaded cattle, sheep, and pigs into pens and cowboys on horseback and on foot dashed back and forth sending their herds in the intended directions. The rodeo wasn't open for the crowds yet. This was the setup.

Trying her best not to stand out, Finny studied the horses in the pens and stayed out of everyone's way. As she moved toward the cattle pens the smell became overwhelming. Finny fought the urge to put her shirt over her nose and mouth. Nothing would make her stand out more than that. After seeing no sign of Joe or Sky, she headed to the barns. Finding a map of the grounds, Finny saw there were over five hundred stalls. Tears burned her eyes suddenly, but she willed them back. She was tired of crying whenever things felt hopeless. Searching just the pens had taken her over two hours. Five hundred stalls would take the rest of the day and time was running out.

She started at barn A; it was empty, as were B and C. Finny changed directions and picked up a run; she'd go high to low. She needed to get them all searched before dark. Joe had told her after dark is when the background, illegal games began. Finny wanted Sky and Joe back well before then.

Barn Y was full of horses, young ones with white tags already glued to their tails, ready for the auction. Finny was able to dash by each stall, all white tags. The next barn the same—sale horses—the next two, all white tags. Finally the tags turned to green. The horses were different, riding horses, rodeo horses, not for sale. Finny checked them all too. She had finished ten barns when what she saw next almost took her to her knees. She staggered back into the barn aisle just in time to stay out of sight.

Joe was forty feet from her with three other men walking in front of the next barn. Finny saw his downcast face. The tallest man was speaking to him in a hushed tone. The other two men stayed right behind them. Finny knew the man with Joe had to be his uncle.

Once they turned the corner she dashed to it just in time to see them slide open a large barn door and go inside. She ran to the other side of the building and came upon a truck with a camper. A chill went down her spine, paralyzing her on the spot. On the truck door, a faded, painted-on sign read "McCoy Livestock." The truck Finny had pictured so often in her nightmares sat right in front of her. It was eerie how similar it was to how she had pictured it, except in her dreams it was always brown. The truck, in reality, was blue.

Finny backed away from the truck and approached the building. She found a small side door. Knowing she was taking a big chance, she entered anyway, desperate to get to Joe. The knob turned and the door was, to her relief, soundless when she opened it. The structure was a giant warehouse for storing farming equipment. Finny slipped in quietly and closed the door behind her.

The building had a large open floor. Several thick poles lining the middle held up the giant roof. Several small offices were built along the sides. There were dozens of large pieces of farming equipment in various stages of repair packed tightly inside, giving her ample places to hide. Finny was halfway to the other side when she spotted Sky with two other horses in a makeshift corral. Her heart somersaulted in her chest as relief flooded through her. He looked okay. Her brain told her to call the police, but what would happen to Joe if she did? His uncle was his legal guardian. Would they help or would it make things worse like Joe feared?

Finny maneuvered to the other side of the building. She wanted to spot Joe again. Slowly and carefully she made her way. Finny could hear men talking. She slid behind a tractor, then got on her belly and crawled underneath.

She found them just outside an empty office. The men were standing around a table. Joe was the only one seated in a chair.

"Let me race, please. I'll run the big horse. I'm not too heavy for him. I'll win you the money back," Joe was pleading.

"Not gonna happen. Besides, it doesn't come close to what you owe me." A tall man came around the table and leaned against it in front of Joe. She knew this was his uncle. "I'm going to ask you one more time. Why is the big horse important to you?" Joe crossed his arms and looked away. Uncle John let out a disappointed sigh, got to his feet, then smashed Joe in the face with his fist, hurling him to the ground. Finny almost screamed; she held her hands over her mouth and choked back a sob.

John turned to his cohorts. "Tie him up." He grabbed his hat off the table then marched out of the building. Finny watched the men drag Joe into an office. They came out moments later and followed John outside. Finny didn't wait for them to get far. She scrambled out from under the tractor and to the office. The door was locked but it was a weak interior door and Finny broke it open on her first try, then dropped by Joe's side. She held his face; he was unconscious and bleeding from a cut on his eyebrow.

"Joe, wake up, please." Finny kissed his forehead and

brushed his hair back. She pulled him to a sitting position and freed his hands, then his feet. Joe began to rouse.

"It's okay, Joe, everything's going be okay."

"Finny, no, you can't be here!" Joe sputtered when he opened his eyes. "He'll hurt you."

Finny kissed him again and draped his arm over her shoulders. "We're going to get Sky and go." She helped Joe to his feet.

"He'll come back. He always wins. He always gets his way."

"That's going to change. Come on, Joe, we're getting out of here."

"If you see him, run."

"Okay."

"Finny, swear to me, you run no matter what."

"You mean no matter what happens to you."

"Yes, promise me."

"Come on, Joe, hurry."

"Promise me!"

"Yes, I promise. Let's go."

The big horse spotted Finny and nickered loudly, pawing the ground. Finny made a makeshift bridle out of a halter and two leads and slipped it over his head. She brought him out of the corral and to the door. "Come on, Joe." He seemed to be out of it, slow to react.

Finny glanced out of the window; all was clear. She opened the door and led Sky out. "Joe, come on, leg me up." Joe did, then swung up behind her. Finny pulled Sky around and headed toward the parking lot.

"We'll ride to the parking lot," Finny said, "then you take the truck and split. I'll ride out and meet up with you in the next town.

"This was too easy, Finny."

"Come on, Joe. It's going to be okay."

"No, it's not." Joe looked around, scanning the area.

"Don't say that. We're getting out of here."

"Don't go for the truck. I don't want him to find out what it looks like or that it even exists."

"Okay, where then?"

"I got to think. He'll find us if we go toward home. We need to hide."

"Let's call the police, Joe. They'll help us."

"Finny, I'll go to juvie 'til I'm eighteen. My uncle promised that if I ever ran, he'd make sure I rotted in there. He'll tell them I'm a chronic runaway, and a thief or anything else he can think of. He's a master con artist. They'll believe him. If they don't, he'll have ten people in an instant backing him up."

"Okay, okay, no police. What about hiding in one of the barns?"

"First place he'd look."

"Joe, he's not a mind reader."

"Go west, that way, toward the ocean. I don't think he'd expect that." The kids made their way behind the sale barn toward the property line. Joe heard a whistle.

"Finny, they're coming."

"They're not, Joe. You're being paranoid." He didn't answer, just looked around but spotted no one.

"Finny, go that way. Through the crowd." Joe pointed toward the walkways intended for people. Finny didn't hesitate; she kicked Sky forward.

"Remember what you promised me, Finny."

"Don't talk like that."

"Promise me!"

"I do, okay." Finny picked up a canter. The crowd was getting thicker and people were beginning to yell in protest at the horse that wasn't supposed to be in the area.

"Joe, we're calling too much attention to ourselves."

"You're right. Head toward the barns. Finny, hand me your phone; they took mine. I'm calling the police."

"What about you?" Finny asked as they ducked into the first barn they came to. Joe didn't get a chance to answer. Up ahead, men began to block the barn aisle. Finny pulled Sky up and turned him around only to find two more cowboys blocking the way they had just come. Joe saw one of the men approaching with a lasso, no doubt to pull them both off the horse. He jumped down. "Finny, when I run at them, you run by and get out of here."

"No, Joe! Get back on, we'll run them down if we have to."

"We'd never make it. These guys can rope Sky's legs out from under him in an instant. Remember you promised me, so be ready, and Finny, call the police as soon as you can. I'm thinking juvie might not be so bad."

Finny broke her promise. She dug her heels into Sky's ribs and sent him bolting toward the man with the rope. The cowboy, caught off guard, staggered back, then jumped out of the way of the massive animal. Finny spun Sky around and looked for Joe.

"Finny, *run!*" Joe screamed at her as he dashed toward the end of the barn. Finny ran at the man trying to cut Joe off. She slid Sky to a stop in front of him, blocking his path, then spun away. Finny looked for the man with the lasso to make sure he wasn't going to take her out. She didn't see him. Joe was clear and he had a good lead. He waved her to follow and dashed around the corner of the barn toward the parking lot. Finny blasted after him, rounded the corner, and found Joe, with the beefy arm of his uncle wrapped tightly around his neck.

Finny heard running footsteps behind her. She spun Sky around as the other cowboys caught up. She looked to Joe, then back to the men.

"Please, Finny," she heard him say. She couldn't do it. She couldn't leave him. She knew Joe wanted her to run, but she loved him, and she couldn't leave him.

"So you must be the reason Joe wanted that big horse back so bad." Uncle John released Joe from the headlock, but left his arm draped over his shoulders.

"Finny, take your horse and go. These men know better than to try and stop you," Joe said plain and steady. He knew it was one thing between him and his uncle as his guardian. If they messed with Finny they could be in a world of trouble.

Finny studied the cowboys around her. Two had disappeared; the remaining three stood back, watching.

"You need to let Joe go."

"Do I?" Uncle John said with a bemused look on his face.

"I'll call the police if you don't."

"Already did, told them they could stop looking for my wayward nephew. He's come home." John gave Joe a painfully tight squeeze.

"That's right, Finny, so now you go home," Joe added, drilling his eyes into hers, telling her to keep her promise.

"Joe, I don't think your little girlfriend here wants to leave."

"She's not my girlfriend."

"Don't you think that's sweet, gentlemen? Young love?" The cowboys around them remained silent.

Joe took a chance and twisted hard, trying to pull out of his uncle's grasp, but it was no use. His uncle was too strong.

"I heard you love to race." Finny's eyes never wavered from Joe's uncle as she spoke.

John raised his eyebrows in surprise. "Did you?"

"Uncle John, she's crazy. Don't listen to her."

"Joe, shame on you to speak so rudely about this nice young lady. And yes, I do enjoy the races. My nephew here used to do a pretty good job."

"You say Joe owes you money, right?" Finny said.

"She sure seems to know a lot, there, Joe, not being your girlfriend and all."

"My horse is real fast. Let Joe race him. He'll win your money back. That's what you want, right? Money?"

"That does sound like fun." Uncle John let out a heavy sigh. "It's too bad Joe's permanently retired from racing."

"I'll race, then." Finny's offer set the cowboys laughing.

"Make her leave, Uncle John, please," Joe begged, desperate.

"I'll run him," Finny continued without missing a beat. "If I win, you get all the money and Joe goes free."

"What do I get if you lose?"

"What do you mean?"

"You heard me, what do I get when you lose? If you're gonna bet me, little girl, it's got to be worth it to me."

"Finny, get out of here now!" Joe's plea fell on deaf ears.

"If I win, you get the money and Joe gets to leave. If I lose, I'll sign my horse over to you. You'll have his papers; you could get double what you could without them."

"Now it's starting to get interestin'."

"Finny, don't trust him. He's a lying sack of crap."

Uncle John wrapped his arm back around Joe's neck and squeezed. He whispered loudly in his ear. "You better get some manners right quick before I lose my temper."

"So is it a deal?" Finny asked, trying not to let her voice quiver, "I win, Joe gets to go and you get the money. If I lose, you get my horse."

"Little lady, you got yourself a deal."

Chapter Twenty-Eight

WORD SPREAD FAST THAT A RACE WAS ON. The unusual twist made it all the more entertaining. Last count, Finny heard there'd be twenty-two racers. She had to fight back nausea from outright terror at what she'd gotten herself into. And Joe? From the look on his face, she didn't know if he'd ever forgive her. The cowboys, so positive of their victory, allowed Finny to ride around the three-mile course so she could chose her path. They were gentlemen, after all. At least that's what Uncle John said with a wicked laugh.

Two hours and the race would begin. It'd be dark, so Finny carefully rode the route the cowboys showed her. She didn't want some unseen obstacle taking them out. Three miles long, it began at the back of the barns, went through the parking lot, and then toward the mountains. Once clear of the parking lot the terrain became hilly, rock-strewn, and full of scrub. Finny had a tough time finding a good path even in the daylight. The half-way point was a bridge where trains passed over the dry riverbed. Once under the bridge, it was a straight path back to the rodeo grounds.

Back at the barn, Finny thought about losing both Joe and her horse. It made her sick. She wouldn't let that happen. She knew the cowboys would underesti-mate her. She was counting on it.

Finny rode back to the starting point. She wanted to stay with Joe until the race but his uncle wouldn't allow it. "He won't let you win," Joe told her as they pulled him away. She took that to heart; she figured if she got out in front and stayed there he'd somehow sabotage her. Finny tried to think like Uncle John, like an evil person. She tried to figure out every scenario he'd try.

Once back to the barn Finny slid off of Sky. She found a stall to put him in so he could eat hay, drink wa-ter, and rest until the race. Finny looked at her watch— little more than an hour to go. She sat and put her face in her hands and said a prayer. She felt like crying but didn't. Oddly, the closer it got to the race the calmer she felt. She looked at Sky. She had every confidence in him. They were a team and they trusted each other, and that made them formidable.

"Are you ready?" Finny looked up when she heard John speak. She stood and grabbed the saddle and bridle she'd brought from the truck.

"Yes, I'm ready. Where's Joe?"

"He's by the finish line. He'll be in charge of taking care of my new horse once you lose."

Finny didn't acknowledge the dig; she knew he wanted to psyche her out. Finny had to steady an agitated Sky as she tacked him. Joe's uncle set him off. The horse's eye never left the man.

"We tried to see what this horse could do, why Joe liked him so much. Figured there was something special about him. But he bucked my rider right off, a rider who broncs for a living." Uncle John let out a big laugh. "Sure caught us by surprise. We knew he wasn't for the rodeo, too big and too old. Didn't know Joe had gotten himself a girl. Explains it all, though. Regular chip off his uncle's block, that Joe."

"He's nothing like you." Finny didn't mean to react, to be baited. Hatred for the man boiled inside her, making her lash out. Her anger just amused John.

"Better get on, girl. Race is about to start."

Finny swung up on Sky and trotted past John toward the starting line. She looked up at the night sky. The moon was half covered by clouds, but it was brighter than last night, and she was grateful for that.

Twenty-three riders total, Finny counted. All men, all adult. They were milling around warming up their horses. The mood was jovial. This was their fun. Finny spotted Joe sitting on the bumper of his uncle's truck with another man standing next to him. She went toward him only to be cut off by another rider.

"Ain't gonna happen, girl. Get in line."

Finny looked at the menacing stranger and turned back. She glanced again at Joe and met his eye. She mouthed, *I love you.* Joe gave her a sad smile. She knew he'd given up. She didn't think he lacked faith in her. He just had too much in his uncle.

"What d'ya say we give the little lady a head start just to be gentlemen?" someone shouted. The crowd murmured in agreement.

"I don't need one," Finny stated, never taking her eyes off Joe. She saw the look of surprise in his face, then his brows furrowed. The crowd laughed at Finny's declaration and the mood became more animated, then intense. It was time.

"Okay, you heard her. Can't say we didn't give her a chance."

Another voice sang out, "Line 'em up!" Within seconds the horses were in what constituted a line in an illegal back-alley race. Finny moved to the middle of the pack, took one more look at Joe, then patted Sky. His ears were perked, his body was tense; he knew the show was on and he felt ready. The whistle blew. Twenty-four horses blasted off into the night.

Sky burst forward underneath her. He was bred to run and his instincts were kicking in. It was all Finny could do to control him. Sky wanted the front. Finny needed the middle, not too fast, not too slow. She watched the riders around her. Some dashed off, and some were purposely hanging back. The first leg of the race was to set pace to get the horses' rhythm. The all-out run would come later. The farther they ran the more the herd thinned. Finny saw she was surrounded, just short of being boxed in by four other riders. She tested her theory by trying to pull out, only to be cut off. A few things went through her mind. Were they that worried about her, or just completely ensuring her loss? She actually found it funny and knew they'd be in for a big surprise. Horses typically don't like hitting each other or banging into things, especially as they run. Sky was a bully—not only didn't he mind, she was pretty sure he liked it.

Finny pulled left, purposely going wide. She heard the men yelling, signaling. It made her smile—going wide was a sure way to lose, but Finny was close to changing course anyway. It was time to get out of the box. She kicked Sky toward the gap. She locked her eye on the cowboy ahead of her, who continually looked over his shoulder to watch her move over. His nine-hundred-pound, 15.2-hand horse didn't know what hit him when Sky, almost twice his size, bashed into his hindquarters and shoved him out of the way. The horse, scrambling hard to stay on its feet, dropped back fast.

Now clear of the box, Sky's rhythm was steady when they hit the dirt parking lot. This was a race of opportunity; your path was your own. Horses were wildly zigzagging between parked cars and around concrete barriers. Finny heard whistles and shouting; she was sure those were signals between the men.

Sky's giant stride opened up underneath her. He was tugging away at her arms, begging her to let him gallop all out. They were approaching the fence that surrounded the parking lot. The other horses ran to the right to the open gate. Finny didn't bother—the fence was less than four feet, a breeze for Sky. He sailed over it. This put her ahead of several of the riders. Again more shouts. Finny was staying wide, not the best route if you planned to win. Several riders were still with her and they shouldn't have been. She realized they were only there to make sure she'd lose. She kicked Sky forward and let him run all out. She hadn't planned on using his remarkable speed, but she knew she had to get far away from those men. She had no intention of letting anyone get close enough to put a rope around her or Sky's legs. She stood in her stirrups and grabbed Sky's mane and kicked him on. It took all she had to hang on as he exploded forward. The men fell behind her quickly and disappeared into the dark.

She was almost to the train tracks now, almost to the pivotal point in her plan. She wasn't going to run the mile down the ravine under the train tracks as intended, then back up on the other side to race home. She was going to cut off more than a mile by jumping over the tracks. Up ahead, right before the ground ended and the bridge began, the mountain was cut away for the train to pass through. The expanse was wide, too wide for any horse, except Sky wasn't just any horse.

Finny pictured him jumping that culvert at Silver Spur, at least fifteen feet, easy. This gap, wide enough for a train, looked almost twice that.

Well ahead of the riders that were out to stop her, Finny knew she had time to line up for the jump. She got to the top and pulled Sky up. She could just make out two riders already down in the ravine, but they weren't going anywhere. That's why she had been allowed to ride her path; they'd watched her so they'd know where she'd go and when to ambush her. She couldn't believe how right Joe was, how devious his uncle was.

Finny trotted Sky to the gap and nudged him toward

it. He went to the edge and stopped hard. He stuck his head down and raked the ground with his hoof several times. Finny used to think this was a sign that he was irritated, but she knew now it was Sky thinking, figuring things out. Finny looked across the divide. It was shockingly big. If they missed, they would fall thirty feet to the tracks below. She pushed that image out of her mind. Sky wouldn't fail. She heard the men coming. She wheeled Sky around and kicked him into a run, stopping several hundred feet from the edge. The men were in plain sight now and coming fast. Finny spun Sky around, slammed him in the sides, and sent him rocketing forward full speed. She heard a train's whistle. To her horror, she saw a train in the distance. She kicked Sky again. They had to make it before the train, before the men got to them. Sky galloped at top speed; wind whistled past Finny's ears, tears streaming from her eyes from the wind and the cold. They were almost to the gap. Finny felt Sky hesitate, then burst ahead. He readied himself—he knew what to do—the train was coming—the whistle was deafening. Sky thundered across the ground until it disappeared and they were flying. Finny went weightless as time slowed down. The train's engine, although near, seemed hundreds of miles away. Finny experienced everything at once: the brilliant sea of stars above, the wind battering her face, the yells and hollers of the cowboys behind her, the scream of the train's whistle, and the stretch of Sky's body as he reached, straining for the other side. The explosion. Finny slammed into Sky's neck, then smashed to the ground when Sky's legs collapsed under him. The big horse flipped on his side and skidded in the dirt. Finny rolled several times before landing in scrub brush, her entire body a spasm of pain. She saw stars, sure it was delirium, then realized it was the night sky.

Finny was desperate for air, desperate for the ability to breathe. She wasn't sure how long she lay there trying—a second, an hour, forever? She rolled over, pushed herself up, and staggered to her feet, only to collapse back to her knees. She tried again and managed to stay standing. Finny looked around, not sure where she was. She looked across the divide; they were on the other side. They'd made it. The noise of the train was slowly fading into the night.

Finny took a step and almost went down again from shock and dizziness. She looked for Sky; he was twenty feet away, standing, head down, shaking. Finny, trying to walk steadily, went to him and picked up his reins. She ran her hands down his legs. He was breathing hard and looking at her. She didn't know what his expression meant. She hoped he hadn't lost his trust, his faith, or his love for her after she'd almost killed them both.

Finny climbed back on. She was so far ahead she could afford a little time. She asked for the canter. He felt slow to respond but his stride was smooth and fluid. Sky was mentally shaken but not physically hurt. Finny picked up the pace. No one was anywhere near her but she didn't care—she galloped full speed to the finish.

Thunderous cheers erupted when Finny crossed the line. People appeared by the dozens, wildly applauding, coming to her and patting Sky, wanting to shake her hand, asking her name. Person after person came up to congratulate her. Finny felt overwhelmed. These people, so against her just minutes ago, had started chanting her name. Mesmerized, she scanned the crowd for Joe.

"Has anyone seen Joe or John McCoy?"

People shook their heads. The other race riders Finny had left in the dust were finally coming in one by one. She saw the first man staring her down. She tensed up, but with this crowd she didn't think he'd do anything. The man rode up, his eyes cold. He took his hat off, stuck his hand out, and said, "Young lady if I live to be a hundred I don't think I'll ever see riding like that again. It was an honor to be beat by you."

Dumbfounded, Finny shook the man's hand. One by one, the other men rode up, removed their hats, and shook her hand. The last cowboy said, "We underestimated you. We deserved to lose."

She thanked them, all while scanning the crowd for any sign of Joe. She asked the last rider, "Do you have any idea where Joe or John McCoy went?" The man stood in his stirrups and surveyed the crowd. His eyes went steely and he sent out an ear-splitting whistle. Within moments six of the other riders were there.

"Anybody see John or Joe?" The cowboy addressed not just the riders but also the crowd.

"John don't like to lose . . . but there ain't no welshin' on a bet here. Let's go find him. I think he needs a reminder on how we do things." The men set off. Finny, not knowing what to do, followed them. They all were heading toward the big barn where Joe had been earlier. Once there, Finny saw the McCoy truck was gone. She felt the blood drain from her body.

"Don't worry yourself, young lady. We don't let no one run out on a bet. We'll find them." Finny saw three of the men were on cell phones, all talking fast while cooling down their horses.

"They got him!" a cowboy yelled and shut his phone. "Trying to leave out of the north exit." Finny nudged Sky forward only to be stopped by one of the cowboys. "Young lady, give us five minutes, then go, okay?" Finny nodded. She didn't know why, but she trusted the man completely. She sat alone on Sky and watched the cowboys, who were now her friends, disappear into the night. She looked at her watch; she waited exactly five minutes and went to the north exit. It took a bit to find it but she did, and Joe was there, waiting under the dim light of the exit sign. Finny slid off of Sky and into his arms. They held each other for a long, long time, each refusing to let the other go. Finny felt warm, loved, and right where she belonged.

"You broke your promise," Joe said, still holding her tight.

"I know."

"You know you must be out of your head, completely crazy, right?"

"Yes, I know that too."

"You know I love you more than anything, right?"

"Yes, I do."

Coda

———

"**Y**ou have a *what?*" Beth asked, astonished.

"Please don't be mad. He was free. I'm working off his board and all his expenses."
Beth pinched the bridge of her nose and let out a sharp breath. "Finny—"

"Before you say anything, Mom, just come look at him. He´s so beautiful and he´s everything I've always wanted!"

Beth turned off the car and stepped out. The displeasure on her face deepened when her new pumps touched the dirt. Finny led her around the new security gate across the Azure Hills driveway.

"He´s perfect to ride, and he jumps the moon," Finny added hoping for a sign of something positive from her mother.

Beth stayed silent as she navigated the ground to keep her shoes out of harm's way. They passed the house and walked up to the stallion pen. Sky blasted out a nicker when he sensed Finny's approach. He stuck his head out of the stall and nickered again when he saw her. Finny rubbed his long neck and looked at her mom. "See, he's perfect . . . Are you mad?"

Beth crossed her arms and kept a nervous distance as she studied the horse.

"He was so skinny and pitiful, I had to take him. I love him so much and I was afraid you'd say no. I know I should have told you . . . asked you."

Something like sympathy flickered in her mother's eyes. Beth took a step toward Sky. "Yes, you should have told me. Owning a horse is a lot of responsibility and a lot of money."

"I know, but I can do this, I swear." Finny tried her best to sound responsible and capable and not like a pleading child.

"Your grades can't suffer. If they do, we will have to rethink this, understand?"

Finny's knees all but buckled with relief, but she still managed to grab her mother in a smothering bear hug. "Oh, Mom, thank you, thank you! They won't suffer, I promise!" Beth let out a laugh and tentatively reached out to touch Sky's nose. Sky gently blew a warm breath on her hand. Beth's smile grew.

"He is beautiful . . . and big." Beth sighed. "I guess I

better give Steven a call and let him know we have another family member."

Finny jumped into her mother's arms again and hugged her with all her might. Beth held her tight. She looked at her daughter. "Finny . . . I know you've wanted a horse for a long time . . . but, money was—"

"Mom, I understand. Really."

Beth kissed the top of her head. "And Finny . . . no more big surprises, okay?" Finny nodded, too overwhelmed to speak.

"Be home by six-thirty for dinner."

"I will. I love you mom."

"I love you too, baby."

Joe waited until Beth´s car had cleared the drive before he stepped out of the feed room.

"You did it and you're still alive," Joe said with a smile.

"Yes, can you believe it?"

"So. When are you going to tell her about me?"